Maybe Forever

a novel

Kim Golden

Echo Books

Stockholm, Sweden

Kim Golden
Echo Books - Stockholm
Gustav III:s boulevard 153
Stockholm, Sweden SE-169 74
kim-golden.com

Publisher's Note: This is a work of fiction. Names, characters, places, and incidents are a product of the author's imagination. Locales and public names are sometimes used for atmospheric purposes. Any resemblance to actual people, living or dead, or to businesses, companies, events, institutions, or locales is completely coincidental.

Cover design: Arijana K./Cover It! Designs
Cover image: 4x6/iStockphoto.com; Svetlana Fedoseyeva/shutterstock.com

Book Layout: ©2014 BookDesignTemplate.com

Maybe Forever/ Kim Golden. -- 1st ed.
ISBN 978-91-981746-4-9

To my one and only muse. You know who you are.
It's always you. It's only you.

CONTENTS

CHAPTER ONE: Laney

Drowning

"Mommy!"

I covered my ears and counted to ten. Slowly...slowly. If I could just stop time for a few moments, get the world to stop spinning so quickly, just one hour...one minute when Liv wasn't chattering...when Freya wasn't shrieking. No, I shouldn't think that way. I shouldn't wish they'd vanish—even if it's temporary. Liv was my heart. My sweet little girl, who needed more than I could give her. And Freya...my angel. Why did I sometimes feel like I didn't love her enough? I bottled this up inside me, corked it tight, hid it deep, deep, deep. I couldn't joke it away. I couldn't shake these baby blues. And I wanted to. I wanted to emerge from the strange, muffling fog shrouding me.

On the other side of the door, Liv was singing to the baby, singing the same song about a fox and what it says, the same song she'd been singing for days. I'd heard it so many times I couldn't take it anymore. I didn't care what the goddamn fox said...I just wanted it to stop...

Soon Mads would be home...or...well, it was hard to tell these days. Sometimes he was home early enough to pick Liv up from daycare. Other times he forgot and I had to rush out with Freya keening and shrieking in her pram and fetch Liv before the daycare teachers got frustrated. At least today he'd texted and said he had meetings. I had to remind myself that soon we'd be celebrating our wedding anniversary and we'd have a babysitter and it would just be the two of us for a while...or maybe not. A message flashed on my screen. "New client wants to celebrate contract signing. Taking all of us from the shop out for drinks. Late tonight. XX"

Liv stopped singing. Now she was at the door again. "Mommy, when is Papa coming home? I want to go to the playground. He said he would take me today."

I groaned. Of course he'd forgotten. He'd promised her at breakfast. As soon as he'd said it, Liv screamed in delight. I wanted to tell him not to make a promise he might not be able to keep. I'd grown up with a father who never kept promises. I swore I would never make promises to my children that I couldn't keep. And I tried my best to do right by them. I wanted them to be happy, I didn't want them to ever doubt that I loved them, even if there were days when I felt like I didn't know why I wanted them. And that was what scared me.

Some mornings I had to talk myself out of staying in bed. Some days I was scared I would walk away from my children. And when I tried to tell my cousin Eddy, she said it was normal. I'm not sure if she took it very seriously. She'd never doubted her love for her twins. But I didn't remember feeling like this when I had Liv. Maybe it was because everything was so crazy then. She was born so prematurely... I'd lost a lot of blood and the doctors were scared they were going to lose us both. And there was a part of me that still had nightmares about the day Liv was born. But I wanted everything to be perfect. I wanted her to have the childhood I never had—one that felt safe, stable...full of love...with parents who wanted to be together, who maybe loved each other a little too much. I wanted her to feel joy. And now I would have to tell her...again...that Daddy wasn't taking her to the playground. Daddy forgot. Daddy had contracts to sign, people to meet.

"Liv..."

"Mommy, does your tummy hurt?"

"No, sweetie, I'm fine. I'll be out in a second."

"When is Papa coming home?"

"Papa's going to be late, so he asked me to take you to the playground."

"But I want Papa."

"I know, sweetie, but he can't do it today." I kept my voice calm and even. She sounded miserable. I knew I ought to open the door and console her but the fallout was what I couldn't handle right now. The tantrum, the kicking, the screaming. She'd curl her little hands into fists and hit me, even as I held her and rocked her and swore to her that Daddy didn't mean to forget, he never meant to forget. It wasn't often that Mads actually had to bear the brunt of Liv's frustration at the broken promises. I was the one who was on parental leave. And some days...some days were like today when nothing went right, when Freya wouldn't stop sleep or Liv demanded my complete attention until her father came home, and then she promptly forgot about me. She saved so many smiles and cuddles for him. And there was a fierceness to his love for his daughters that was so beautiful and wonderful...and sometimes I felt outside the scope of it. Stupid, I know. I knew he loved me. He told me every day, and when neither of us was exhausted from the constants of life we showed one another. It's just...no, I had to remember I wanted this. Wasn't this what had catapulted us into our relationship in the first place? I was so gung-ho to have a baby. A baby with Niklas, not Mads...but then Mads came into the picture and I knew. I knew he was the one I was supposed to have my babies with. He was the one I was supposed to wake up to every morning. So why did it feel so strained now? Why did it seem like—in the grand scheme of his life—there was no space for me anymore?

Liv shrieked and kicked the door. "Mommy! Mommy! I want Papa!"

I took a deep breath and sighed. God...if I weren't still breast feeding I would pour myself a large glass of white wine and sit on the balcony... It was still nice out, I ought to take Liv and Freya out again for fresh air, maybe she'd calm down...maybe she'd be okay with—

My phone beeped again. I swiped the screen. Another message from Mads.

Going to design forum in Milan in two weeks with Jonas + Benny. Presenting our latest ideas + talking about organic design. Will be there Thurs-Sun.

That Saturday was our anniversary. Four years of marriage. We'd already arranged to borrow Henrik's beach house and spend a grown-up weekend there. Eddy and Henrik had already agreed to take the kids for the entire weekend... I texted him back: "But that's our anniversary."

"I'll call you later."

I cast the phone down on the tile floor. It skittered across the dark grey tiles and bounced to a stop at the edge of the tub. Outside the door, Freya had now joined Liv in crying. Their sobs were my Greek chorus, alerting me of my status as a mom. Status update? Shitty. I wished I could get through a day without bursting into tears. I wished I could actually finish the errands I had without constantly having to stop, to be able to remember that I needed to go to the grocery store before I was already trying to cook dinner. I needed help. I needed...Mads.

I couldn't hide in the bathroom forever. I pushed myself up and opened the door. Liv was on the floor, kicking her bare foot on the gallery wall. Her pale yellow sundress was grubby now from the juice she'd spilled on herself at lunchtime. Her wild brown curls formed a halo around her face. She was still crying, devastated that her father was not going to do as he'd promised. I picked her up and held her close. At first she squirmed and resisted me. She pushed at me and kept repeating "*nej*"—the Danish child's version of "no," and a word I was more than familiar with from the great joy Liv often took in turning it into a song. It didn't take long for her to stop struggling. She flung one arm around my neck and rested her cheek against mine.

We walked down the hall to the room she shared with Freya. The ceiling fan whirred above us, keeping the room cool in the wet summer heat. Freya's nap had lasted all of fifteen minutes and she looked furious at even being put in her crib. As soon as she saw me she stopped crying and stretched out her arms to me. Liv was quiet now too. She let out a little sigh and murmured against my cheek, "I want Daddy."

"I know, sweetie..." I kissed her and brushed a single curl from her damp face. "So do I."

* * *

Liv calmed down enough that I managed to convince her we'd go to the playground together and have Mommy-and-Liv time. She sulked but accepted this change of plans. I even managed to convince her to trade her favorite sundress for a T-shirt and shorts. The dress was too grubby for going out in public. And though many of our neighbors were also parents of small children, their children always managed to look like little fashion plates while mine sometimes looked as though they'd dressed themselves. Most times I didn't care but there'd been a few times when people had commented on Liv's "eclectic style" and the tone of voice was enough to cue me that they thought she looked terrible. I didn't mind that Liv often wanted to wear bright yellow tops with green and red striped pants or that she hated wearing matching socks. More often than not, she came home from daycare missing a shoe. I was used to this.

At the playground, she spotted two of her friends from daycare. I knew she wanted to play with them but she stuck close to me. I was sitting in the shade of the chestnut tree, trying not to think too much about the state of my marriage. How could it be that I had everything I wanted but I still felt lonely? As much as I loved Mads, it often seemed like the spark between us was sputtering. He was distracted; I was constantly juggling the kids.

I waved to the children and encouraged Liv to play with them. "But you'll be alone," she said.

"I won't be alone," I assured her. "Freya's here with me."

Liv considered this. She was so like her father. They shared so many mannerisms. She bit her lower lip when she smiled, just as he did—especially when he was trying to charm the pants off you. Then she did a little dance and informed me that Emelie—who was her best friend from *dagpleje*, the Danish version of daycare—was in the sandbox. I encouraged her to go and say hello, which she finally did. She skipped over and soon was ensconced in their favorite made-up game of Princess Takes the Castle.

Emelie's mother was deep in conversation with another of the neighborhood moms. Normally I would have joined them but I wasn't in the mood. I didn't want to be pulled into their gossip session. I just wanted to enjoy this quiet moment with Freya, who'd fallen asleep during the walk over. Her hair was damp with perspiration. I had a washcloth with me, which I'd soaked in cold water and stuck in a plastic bag. I took it out and gently swabbed her neck and forehead. She made a tiny noise in her sleep. I loved these moments...when Freya was sleeping peacefully, no crying, just contentment. I watched how her lips puckered and calmed in her sleep...how her tiny hands balled into fists then relaxed. Sometimes when I watched her, she reminded me of the baby pictures my mother had kept in her wallet. Pictures of me, my eyes wide and dark as a roe deer. Her skin was not as light as Liv's. Freya was darker, a golden brown like a perfect piece of oak.

I don't know when I fell asleep. Maybe it was the heat of the sun beating down on my skin. Maybe it was my insomnia. I couldn't sleep. Freya woke up too often. After we'd got her used to sleeping in her own bed, she'd now started waking two or three times a night. Mads usually slept through it. But I never slept deeply enough. I'd wake at the slightest sound. Afraid that somehow

Freya had climbed out of her crib and fallen...or that perhaps I'd forgotten to lock the door...I was scared all the time of my own...inadequacies.

For a second, I couldn't remember where I was. I looked around—Liv and Emelie were no longer in the sandbox—Freya...no, she was still in her stroller. Still sleeping as peacefully as she rarely did at night.

I grabbed the handle of the stroller and jogged forward, hoping the jostling wouldn't wake Freya. I called out for Liv. I raced along the path, calling out for her until I saw her on the swings with Emelie. Her friend's mother was pushing them both. Elinor, Emelie's mother, waved at me. When I was close enough she called out, "Did you get the text? I saw you were sleeping and I didn't want to wake you. You looked like you needed a break."

I shook my head. "I...I didn't hear it."

"She's safe as houses." Elinor laughed. I tried to laugh as well. Liv and Emelie were screaming with delight the higher Elinor pushed them. But all I kept thinking was that I'd nearly lost her.

* * *

I lost track of time. Liv grew tired of playing in the sandbox and came over to me. She held my hand as we walked to the grocery store, bought groceries and then went home. But somehow by the time we got home, Liv changed her mind about the day we were having and began to cry again. I tried to give both her and Freya dinner but it didn't work. I ended up with two very unhappy little girls again. My phone rang again. It was my boss Jens. He'd already tried to call me several times but I'd been too busy to answer. "It sounds like you're in the thick of things with being a mom," he joked.

"Well, I've got my hands full." Liv was underfoot, trying to climb in my lap while I tried to navigate my phone and my laptop. I shushed her and told her to go and play with Freya, but she stomped an imperious foot on the floor and barked out a resounding "*nej*." On the other line, Jens cleared his throat. "Sorry, Jens, it's the post-dinner tantrum hour here."

"Ah, well, maybe you'll be interested in what's going on."

"Intrigue at the office?"

"I told you last week how they're talking about restructuring. Well, now it looks like they meant it. They're evaluating all the teams, looking to see which ones scored highest among clients in terms of how smoothly the projects went, the client and end-consumer feedback on the work they created, etc."

I nodded and tried to keep an eye on Freya, who was now at that stage of development where she was scooting and scrawling everywhere. I watched her wiggle from the living room to the hallway leading to the bedrooms.

"I'm guessing they're looking at sales figures, too." I left my chair and followed Freya's wonky trail to her bedroom. I knew she was looking for her stuffed penguin. It was her favorite toy, the one she refused to sleep without. I usually kept it on the bottom shelf of the set of floating shelves we'd installed in the girls' bedroom. Mads had moved it to a higher shelf, and now Freya was staring up at it with the sort of longing that could erupt into tears again at any moment. I grabbed Mr. Penguin, as we called the toy, and put it a few meters away from Freya. She immediately reached for it, happy again. "And my team's projects have always netted great results."

"Well, that's why I'm calling," Jens said. His voice sounded muffled against the layer of background noise—espresso machines hissing, snippets of conversations tumbling over one another, clanging glasses. "We want to keep your team...you, Marius, Johan...together. But it'll only work if you come back a little earlier."

"I can't do that..." I said it before I even thought it through. I couldn't leave Freya yet, even if there were days when the fog around me made me wonder how much I truly loved my baby. I told myself I'd love her more, and sometimes I felt like I did. Even today...when she'd cried so much her cheeks flamed red...deep down, I knew I loved her like there was no tomorrow. "It's too soon."

"Laney, you had to start your maternity leave early again...you've been away for almost a year now," Jens reminded me...as if I needed reminding. I'd gone into labor early again, had been in labor for close to fourteen hours before Freya finally arrived. "And the guys at the top...they need to see you are serious about your career."

"I thought I'd already proven that to them."

"Their memories are short. If they don't see you, they think you don't want to play the game."

"I need to think about this. I need to talk to Mads as well—"

"It's not his career, Lanes. It's yours."

"He's my husband, Jens. Of course I'm going to talk to him about this."

"You remember when you moved to Copenhagen? You made the decision without even talking to Niklas," Jens pointed out. "This is no different. It's your career, Lanes, not his. And if you still want a job at the end of the day, you're going to have to decide who and what you prioritize."

"My kids will always come first."

"Just think about it, Laney. I'm giving you two weeks to think about it. I've got to tell them by mid-August if you're coming back."

"I'll think about it."

"Think hard, Lanes. We'd rather have you back than have to let you go."

* * *

As soon as he arrived home, the mood transformed. My little girls forgot about me. Freya squealed with delight as soon as she heard his voice. She wiggled out of my arms and crawl-scooted across the floor to him. Liv danced around him, singing, "Daddy's home, Daddy's home!" And Mads...well, he loved his girls. He scooped them both up and kissed them, bounced them around and told them how he'd missed them all day. Watching him with them sometimes made me forget about how lately he was more absent than present. He spoke Danish with them, and Liv, who sometimes stumbled over simple English words, kept up with him. With me, she spoke a combination of English and Danish. And she wrinkled her nose at English words she thought were weird. But with Mads, she danced and sang in Danish, her eyes alight with so much love for her father that it made me ashamed to feel any ounce of jealousy. My daughter had what I'd wanted all of my life—a father who adored her, who would probably do anything for her.

I waited until it was my turn. Once Liv had decided she'd had enough of her father's snuggles with his razor-stubbled cheeks and chin, she wriggled down to the floor and ran off to look for Bobbi Fox. With Freya still crooked in his arm, he reached for me with his free hand and pulled me close. I turned my face up to be kissed but it was quick, not the lingering one I wanted. "Sorry I'm so late," he said and then planted a kiss on my lips. "The Vesterbrogade team wanted to meet and talk more about the hotel project."

"It's okay," I assured him. I kept my arms around him and leaned into his chest. Freya's chubby hand patted the top of my head. His shirt smelled hot and damp from outside. Traces of smoke, sawdust and beer clung to the cotton. "I saved some dinner for you, if you're hungry."

"Starving..." And then he kissed me again, another quick peck, before he too wriggled away in search of food.

I trailed behind him, feeling a lot like a groupie following the rock star whose touch she lives for. Four years. Four years and two children and he hadn't changed. He still looked as disarming and sexy as when we first met. A few strands of gray shimmered in his red-gold hair, but Mads still looked exactly as I remembered from that Copenhagen Cryo video. His body was still lean and firm. Every muscle still so perfectly honed that I often wondered how he could even be real. Women still approached him, still flocked to him. And he pretended not to see, not to notice. But sometimes I wondered if it secretly pleased him. To be so desired, to still be so in demand. No wonder the clinic had wanted to sue us...

I, on the other hand, was not as slender and toned as I'd been before the babies came. A c-section scar ran across my belly from giving birth to Liv. I'd been afraid I'd have to have another caesarean with Freya but she was a natural birth. I was still trying to lose my baby weight. I'd gained fifteen pounds with Freya. Fifteen pounds that seemed to settle around my hips and thighs. I tried jogging, dieting...nothing seemed to shake it, but Mads claimed to prefer me curvy. I wasn't sure I believed him. I wanted to, but whenever I looked in the mirror I saw a washed-out, lackluster version of myself. I tried to make up for it by still doing all the things that made me feel sexy—wearing makeup, getting my hair done, getting a bikini wax even when I knew I'd be too tired to give Mads enough time to even enjoy it. We hadn't made love in months. He was still affectionate with me...but he didn't initiate lovemaking now. And I didn't try. He still kissed me with the same passion, still nuzzled into me at night and claimed me with his hands, but...I wanted more. And I didn't know why he was so disinterested.

He was already at the table, eating the chicken and salad I'd prepared while cradling Freya. "Sit with me, *kareste*."

I joined him at the table and took Freya so that he could eat more easily. Once she'd settled into me, I asked him about Milan.

"It's a forum or some kind of exhibition on new Scandinavian design. They've invited twenty designers and firms to take part in it." He fetched a bottle of beer from the refrigerator and twisted it open. "You know how good this feels? They think we are part of this new wave of Nordic design. They're comparing us to Fritz Hansen, Arne Jacobsen and Bruno Mathson." His heroes—the icons of Danish design. He was bristling with pleasure at being compared with the likes of them. And he really was that good. The pieces he designed for us were proof of it.

"It's our wedding anniversary, though..."

"So come to Milan. We can celebrate there."

"We've tried that before." I picked at the extra napkin on the tabletop, fraying the edges with my nails. "It's always the same at these fairs and forums. You'll be so busy, you won't have time to spend with us...and traveling with a seven-month-old and a four-year-old..."

"I'm doing this for us, Laney. I'm doing this so you and the girls won't have to worry about—"

"We have what we need. We don't need more." I didn't want to have this argument again—every now and then Mads still felt like he had to compete with my old life. Even if it would have been wonderful to have that sort of financial security, I didn't want the emotional void that came with it. I could live with saving up for the vacations we took and dreaming of the summer house Mads kept talking about but that we couldn't afford.

"I'm not just doing this for you. I'm not a fucking failure, Laney—"

"I didn't say you were a failure!" Freya was getting agitated. I didn't want her to start crying, so I took her to her bedroom and put her in her crib with her penguin. Liv was sitting on the floor by her bed with her stuffed fox.

"Why is Papa mad?" she asked me in a hushed voice. She was cradling her fox, holding it like it was her very own baby. "Is he mad at me?"

"No, Livvie. Papa is just tired..." I pulled back the top sheet and got her into bed. "I promise, he'll come in soon...he'll read your favorite story." I breathed a relieved sigh as Liv climbed into her bed without a barrage of questions.

"Tell Papa I want the story about the fox."

"I'll tell him."

I closed the door when I left the girls' room. Mads was still in the kitchen. He'd abandoned his plate of food and was standing by the sink, his hands braced on either side of it.

"I don't want to fight, Mads..."

"Like hell you don't."

"And now Liv thinks you're mad at her..."

"Don't do that, Laney—don't make this about the kids."

"I'm just telling you what she said to me—"

"This design forum—fucking hell, Laney, it's good for me and the guys. We've worked so hard trying to get established and now we're there. I thought you wanted this too."

"I wanted you to get the level of success you said you wanted. You said you didn't want to *be* the *new* Bruno Mathson, you said you just wanted to make beautiful furniture—and that's what you do."

"I want us to never have to worry—"

"We don't have to worry. We're fine..."

"I want you to have the things you want—"

"I want my husband, then! I don't want to feel like a single mom all the time. I need you here, I need you!"

Mads shook his head and stalked out of the kitchen. I followed him, my insides twisting and tying in knots. "I told Liv you would read to her...."

"I will! Jesus Christ, I read to her every night, Laney—don't you start saying I'm not here for my daughters..."

"I need you here for me too—"

"I can't be here 24-7, Laney, they need my help at the workshop too—"

"Mads, listen to me...my boss—they want me to come back to work—"

"Isn't that what you want?"

"What? No, not yet—"

"You're always saying you're bored being at home, so go back to work."

"I'm not bored, I never said I was bored." I couldn't remember saying it, but maybe I had. Sometimes I missed being around other adults. I didn't want to sit through another play date with a Danish version of a latte mamma who was perfectly content to talk in that sing-song baby voice. I missed talking to my husband about something other than what the kids had done all day. I missed having a life that was just mine.

He raked his hands through his hair. We were sinking—*I* was sinking. And I watched him as if through a blurred window, watched the tension steeling his shoulders, the taut pull of his jaw as he paced and tried to figure out how to untangle this mess.

"Laney...just, leave the kids with Ingrid and Anton, or see if Henrik and Eddy can take them, and come to Milan with me."

"You know it won't work. You'll be too busy..."

"Laney, I want you to come."

"I know."

"But you won't."

"How will you make sure we have time together? I want to be alone with you."

"I don't know what you want me to do."

"Carve some time out for me. I need you too, Mads. I'm floundering here. I'm trying to keep everything running so you don't have to focus on what's going on here."

"I'm here every night—"

"You're here, but you're not here. Your mind's on the workshop, on your projects. I try to talk to you and you don't hear me. You make promises to Liv—she was so upset because you forgot you promised to take her to the playground...and I've been trying to cover for you when you tell her you're going to do things and then you don't—"

"I didn't promise her we'd go to the play—"

"You promised her at breakfast, and she remembered it. She remembers *everything* you tell her, Mads. She *never* forgets." My hands dropped to my sides. My insides twisted, coiled, pulled so hard... I was shaking so hard, I felt as though I'd lose my footing if I kept standing. I sank onto the sofa and then breathed in and out slowly. My chest felt hot and tight.

Mads stopped pacing. He came over to me, sat beside me and rubbed the back of my neck with his strong fingers. "*Tag det roligt, Laney. Det er okay. Vi vil være okay.*" He pulled me close to him. My body betrayed me. It gave in so easily to him. Even when he was part of the reason I felt so awful. I wanted to be able to look at him and list in the most rational tone of voice all the ways he was failing me. I wanted him to understand that just kissing me wouldn't magically solve our problems.

"Tomorrow...we'll celebrate our anniversary tomorrow," Mads cupped my cheek with his hand. He bit his lower lip and smiled at me. I nodded slowly. The pain in my chest eased enough that breathing didn't hurt now. I hated these spasms...they were happening more and more now. Whenever I was too upset or anxious... God, my hands were still shaking. Mads noticed, too. He clasped my hands between his. We sat like that, neither of us looking at the other, until finally my pulse stopped roaring in my ears. "I'll book a table for us at Madklubben. I'll call Ingrid and see if Sasha can come and watch the girls overnight. And then I'll book a room for us at the Kong Arthur...and it can be like that first night we spent together. Okay...? Just you and me, *elskede*. No distractions."

I nodded again. I would take this. I knew this would have to do until he could finally take some time off from work.

We sat like this, with him still holding my hands but not looking at me. And me...I just nodded and then said, "Don't forget to go in to Liv..."

Mads murmured "okay" and then let go of my hands. He kissed the top of my head, then left me on the sofa. I heard him as he spoke to Liv; my heart swelled as I listened to the loving tone he used with her. I cleaned up the kitchen, then turned off the lights. I waited in the bedroom for him to come and lay down beside me. But finally I couldn't keep my eyes open any longer. I didn't hear him creep in and turn off the bedside lamp. I didn't feel his weight in bed beside me.

When I woke the next morning, he'd already gone to the workshop.

CHAPTER TWO: Mads

Make It Up to Her

She was right.

Of course she was. Sometimes I told myself I couldn't expect Laney to carry the burden on her own. Other times I took for granted how strong she seemed. I'd seen how she handled Liv and Freya—even on the worst of days she was capable of doing it all without me. And maybe that was the worst of it. I knew she'd be fine without me.

All of this was coursing through my mind as I crossed the bridge to the city. A wispy layer of clouds blurred the sky. Though it was still early, heat rose from the pavement and through the soles of my shoes. It looked to be another one of those sticky summer days that Laney always called "dog days." I was already sweating even though I tried not to walk too fast. The first week of July...just a week until my wedding anniversary and Laney and I were fighting. My wife...even at our low points I was still so happy I could call her that, that she'd chosen me...my wife... even if, right now, she wasn't very pleased with me. I would have to figure out a way to make it up to her. I needed to unravel whatever was going on inside of her. I missed my wife who would reach for my hand and lace her fingers with mine over dinner. I missed how she'd lower her eyes...those coppery-brown eyes of hers that sometimes mystified me...and slowly, slowly lick her lips and curve them into a smile that promised so many things. I missed how she'd call me into the bedroom and I'd find her naked and waiting, tempting me to be late for meeting Anton and Adam for a beer or going to the gym. And she always won out...I could never resist her pull on me.

I loved Laney. It was that simple. I needed to tell her that. I left without even touching her or kissing her. I never did that... I stopped in my tracks. I was halfway across the bridge. I could go back. I could tell her I was sorry about last night. I'd fallen asleep while reading to Liv. We barely made it through *Hvad Betyder Ræven?* When I woke, it was already six in the morning and the sunlight streaming in the window made the room feel like an oven, even with the ceiling fan whirring above us. But Liv still slept peacefully, her thumb planted firmly in her mouth. And Freya...my littlest angel...was cooing in her sleep. I'd stood over her, watching the slow, even breaths she took as her chubby fingers twitched. Whatever Laney and I were going through, we would figure it out. We had to. I didn't want to lose my family. I didn't want to lose my wife. I didn't want to lose her.

I turned around and started heading back to our building. I still had enough time to go back and make things right and get to the workshop in time for the design meeting Anton had scheduled. He'd quit teaching last year and joined us after three years of hanging around and helping us build a fair share of cabinets and shelving units. And though he wasn't always a deft hand at carpentry, he made up for it with his expertise at organization. He ran the office, he made sure invoices were paid on time, and he was often the first point of contact. I was back on Sortedam Dossering when my phone vibrated. I pulled it out of the back pocket of my jeans. It was a text from my cousin Henrik, reminding me we needed to check in on *farmor*. Then another text came, this one from Anton—our first client was early. Shit... I was only two blocks from the apartment. I wanted to sprint home, even if I only got five minutes with Laney. But there wasn't time.

I'd make it up to her later.

I wasn't sure which of the guys had recommended Benny to us, but she was a distraction. Every year we took in a couple of interns from *Designskole* to help them get practical experience and lighten the load for us. This year we had three—Willem, Ibrahim and Benedikte, or Benny, as she kept telling us to call her. She looked more like a pinup from the 1950s than a furniture designer. She showed up every day in overalls that only enhanced her assets and deep red lipstick that made her full lips even more obvious. Looking at her was like seeing her naked. And her direct stare—she always stared and her lips curled into this cheeky smile that challenged you. No, she was trouble. She was good at what she did. There was no question about that, but she was one of those women who knew how to push buttons, how to make you feel unsettled. Jonas had already confessed to me over beers that he had his eye on her. He was newly single and on the look-out for someone who'd fill the void in his life left by his ex-wife.

I ducked my head at her as I came into the workshop. She was staining a dining table Jonas had designed. Her fingertips were bruised a reddish brown that reminded me of blood. "*Hej*, Mads," she called out to me. I said a quick hello; I didn't want to linger. The summer heat hadn't permeated the thick stone walls yet, but soon we'd have to open the windows.

Anton was already in the office we'd set up at the back of the workshop. Before, it was my storage area, but with the demand growing for our furniture designs, Jonas and I decided we needed to get more organized. Laney helped us initially, but then Anton joined us and took on the task of setting order to our daily lives.

"I made you some coffee," he said without looking away from the computer screen. He gestured towards the coffeemaker. "And don't forget to book the restaurant."

"How do you know about that?"

"Ingrid told me, so Laney must have told her." Anton shrugged. The keys on the keyboard clicked and clacked.

I poured myself a cup of coffee. "Mads, maybe you should skip the forum."

"Did Laney put you up to this?"

"No, but maybe she should have."

"Don't, Anton. I already got into it with her last night."

Anton finally looked away from the screen. He reached for his coffee mug. "She's not herself these day, Mads. I noticed it last time you two were round. She's...it's like the life's been sucked out of her."

"She's just tired. Freya's not sleeping again."

"I think it's more than that." Anton scratched his neck. "I've known Laney a long time—"

"I know."

"Mads—just...follow through, okay?" Something in his tone of voice caught me off guard. His dark eyebrows were knitted together, the line of his shoulders tense. "She needs this."

Anton's words kept eating away at me. I knew Laney wasn't happy. I didn't know what to do to make her happy. She always looked...worried, and when I tried to talk to her about it, we ended up arguing. And I saw how worn out she looked. And I pretended not to see. Oh fuck, this was my fault. I knew it. I could have been better at being so many things for her. And she stuck with me. She still told me she loved me even if sometimes her voice sounded so weary that I was afraid to question, even in jest, if she was certain. Because why would she be certain? I'd not been there for her, not since Freya was just a couple of months old. I'd helped as long as I thought she needed it and then jumped right back into working.

I called the restaurant and booked a table, then I called the hotel and asked them for one of the spa suites. Then I texted Laney...told her how much I loved her and to meet me at the restaurant at 7:30.

Tonight I would make it up to her.

Tonight I would get everything right.

"I heard it's your anniversary."

I looked up from the sketches Jonas had given me. Benny was perched on the far end of the farm table we used for all meetings and group pow-wows. "It's actually next week, but we'll all be in Milan."

"So you're celebrating early?" She crossed her ankles. Her overalls gapped at the side and revealed glimpses of evenly tanned skin. I glanced away. "I love that you two are so...romantic." She said it as though my wanting to do something nice for Laney was quaint.

"Did you finish the updates to the sketches for the Hotel Alexandra project?" I didn't want to discuss Laney with Benny. I knew how it would go. Benny was one of those women who said she was one of the guys. But she made sure you always knew she wasn't one of the guys. And right now I couldn't concentrate with her watching me, swinging her legs back and forth, flashing that smile I knew my workshop mates Jonas and Morten had called saucy. Saucy because she made you feel like she'd stripped you naked without even removing a single piece of clothing, like she should see past all your defenses. She was the sort of woman you could fuck if you wanted and pretend you could go back to being friends. Because that's what the cool girls did. At least, that's what Laney used to tell me. Because she said she'd been one of those women.

I stole another glance at Benny. She'd hopped off the table and was now peering down at the table top and the unfurled prints of the ideas for the hotel renovation we'd presented for a project bid. She leaned forward, the tops of her breasts suddenly exposed. I felt my mouth going dry. I looked away. I didn't want her. I knew I didn't. I wanted my wife. But...no, this was just a rough patch. Benny was not the one I wanted to hold.

I wanted Laney.

I wanted her to want me again.

CHAPTER THREE: Laney

Is This It?

I was tempting fate, wearing this dress. It was the dress I'd worn for him so many years ago. I'd found it at the back of my closet, wrapped in tissue paper and safely hidden away in a garment bag. I'd pulled it out for nostalgia's sake. I could still remember when I'd found it in Eddy's boutique. I'd imagined an entire history for this wisp of a dress. And when I wore it that first time, I'd felt as beautiful as the dress—delicate, a little mysterious. What I couldn't believe was that it still fit. Two pregnancies had changed my body. My hips were a little wider now and my breasts heavier, but the dress still skimmed my curves and the Laney I saw in the mirror was...desirable, maybe even beautiful. I turned to see how it looked from the back—was that my ass? It looked like a peach waiting to be devoured—a J-Lo ass...a Beyoncé ass...how could that be my ass? Or was chasing after a four-year-old and a seven-month-old better exercise than all the jogging I used to do? I smiled at my reflection—I almost looked like the old me. I almost felt like the old me—getting excited to see Mads, knowing that in a few hours we could be making love and we wouldn't be interrupted by toddlers waking up and wanting snacks or four-year-olds who suddenly remember they want to tell us what Bobbi Fox had to say today... I would have Mads to myself again, even if it was only for one night.

Sasha, Anton and Ingrid's eldest daughter, was doing babysitting duty. She'd already charmed Liv into taking a bath—no mean feat since my little charmer didn't mind being covered in mud or sweat—and changing into a nightshirt. Now she was reading to Liv and Freya—thankfully she'd managed to convince Liv that *What Does the Fox Say* was all well and good but *Cat in the Hat* was much more fun. Sasha had come by earlier so that I could go to the salon and get the full package—hair cut and pretty much full-body wax maintenance. I hadn't done any of that since Freya was born. She was not a calm baby, though now she was being the perfect little cherub, sitting in Sasha's lap, clapping along with the sing-song rhythm of Sasha's voice as she kept both girls enthralled with what the Cat would do next.

I slipped into a pair of the come-fuck-me heels I hadn't worn since the beginning of my pregnancy. Just putting them on made me feel like suddenly I was sexy and wanton. I practiced walking in them, remember Eddy's advice from when we were teenagers—swing your hips, don't stalk...that's the whole point of heels...to get them looking in the right place. That old familiar feeling returned. I wobbled at first and then with each step I took my body remembered the right way to walk, the right way to sway.

I grabbed my clutch and my shawl and crossed the hall to the girls' room. Sasha whistled at me. "Damn! *Du ser godt ud!* I love that dress, Aunt Laney!"

"Mommy, you look bee-yoo-tee-ful!" I bent down so Liv could give me a kiss. She giggled and ran her fingertip along the embroidered hem. "You look like a princess, Mommy."

"Why thank you, sweetie. Do you think Daddy will think so too?"

She nodded. "Daddy says you're the prettiest woman in the whole world."

I gave her a good cuddle, then kissed Freya goodbye.

Hopefully tonight we could get back on track.

He was late. I didn't want to glance at my phone again. I didn't need to. The waitress had already come by twice asking if I wanted to order a starter while I waited for my guest. I shook my head no and asked for another glass of wine. I was on my second glass. I'd had to drink slowly to make sure I wouldn't overdo it. Please let him be on his way. Please let him not be in an accident or stuck in another meeting. My mind was already rationalizing the reasons he wasn't here.

I was at the last possible one—he forgot—when my phone beeped. I swiped the screen.

Running late—there in 15 minutes. XOXO.

I typed in "OK" and took another sip of my wine. He was on his way. He hadn't forgotten me. But then the minutes crept by and fifteen minutes bled into thirty minutes. I texted him but received no reply. I waited a few more minutes and tried not to let my spirits fade. I knew how he was when he was at the workshop. He could get caught up in a project, new ideas would come to him, seducing him away from thoughts of anything else. I tried texting again but he still didn't answer.

It was over an hour now. I flagged down the waitress, made a ridiculous excuse that I was certain she saw through, and paid for my drinks. When I walked out of the restaurant, I'd hoped I'd bump into him, but he was nowhere to be found on Store Kongensgade. Though it was nearly nine o'clock in the evening, the sky wasn't dark. Summers in Scandinavia were magical like that. The white nights...the strange, disconnected feel from the rest of the year. I tried to stay focused on this as I walked the route that would take me to his workshop. There was no point in going to the hotel. If he'd forgotten about the restaurant, there was no way he'd show up at the hotel.

That old familiar feeling? Where I felt beautiful and sexy and desirable? It was seeping away, taking with it every morsel of my self-confidence. Was I so easy to forget? Even when I'd told him I needed him... I nearly began sobbing as I waited for the traffic light to go from red to green. I blinked the tears back. No, I would not cry. I was not going to be one of those women who became hysterical in public, even if my stomach was twisting in knots and my eyes burned. Fuck! This was embarrassing...

By the time I arrived at his workshop, I'd talked myself down, told myself I could forgive him for forgetting about me as long as he was creating something beautiful. His passion for his craft was one of the things I loved about him...even when it meant his craft was more like his mistress. I put on a practiced smile, reminded myself that there were worse things that could happen... I'd nearly convinced myself that I was no longer angry when I finally pushed open the door and took in the scene. The atmosphere was more party than meeting... Music blasted from the ceiling speakers. The main area—what they usually used as a showroom/consultation area was crowded with bodies... Somewhere in here was Mads. I eased past the unfamiliar bodies, until I saw him...leaning against the farm table they jokingly referred to as their roundtable, beer in hand, and laughing at something the woman with him was saying. At first I didn't recognize her but then it clicked—this was the infamous Benny, the bombshell Jonas spent ages swooning over when we'd had a barbecue in our apartment building's communal garden. She tossed her hair back and reached out—her hand lingered on his arm. *Move, Mads,* I wanted to scream. *Don't let her touch you!* But he took a swig of his beer and let her hand stay perched near his elbow. She took a step closer to him—his eyes traveled the whole length of her and then lingered on her chest.

Fucking hell...

I shouted his name, hoping he could hear me above the music and conversations. I was nearly there when he finally turned and saw me. I didn't imagine the startled look on his face. He rushed over to me, already apologizing even though I could barely hear him over the music. He took my arm and led me through the crowd again. When we were outside, he tried to explain again.

"You could have called me." I stepped away from him. "You should have said you were having a party at the workshop."

"It was spur of the moment—we won the bid for the hotel project. And the owners sent everything...the drinks, the food...by courier." He blocked me in by the wall. "Laney, I'm sorry...I should have..."

"You should have come. You should have remembered what you said last night." I dodged the kiss he tried to give me, it landed on the side of my mouth. I pushed him away. "No, you can't kiss or fuck your way out of this one..."

"Jesus, Laney, I'm sorry! I didn't mean for this to happen, we just got so excited when we heard the news."

I shook my head; I didn't want to hear any more. "I'll see you at home."

"*Fanden*, Laney...don't just walk away."

But I kept walking. I told myself he'd catch up with me. He'd come home, we'd work everything out. But by the time I crossed the bridge, I knew he wasn't behind me.

He'd let me go.

* * *

I sent Sasha home in a taxi. She didn't ask the obvious. Instead, she simply told me the girls were already asleep, and then gave me a tight hug before she skipped downstairs to the waiting taxi. I stepped out of my heels and left them by the front door. Barefoot now, I padded down the hallway and checked on Liv and Freya. They were both fast asleep. Liv had thrown off the bed sheet and was sprawled across her bed. Her stuffed fox had fallen on the floor. I crept into the room and picked up the fox, then tucked it into the bed. Sasha had left the window open enough to catch the breeze. Freya had her penguin in one hand while her thumb was planted firmly between her lips. I stroked her burnished curls... my god, how could he give me two daughters, such gifts of love, and still make me feel like there was no love left between us?
I whispered goodnight to my sleeping daughters and then backed out of the room.

I wasn't sure how long I sat on the sofa, waiting...my face stripped of all the makeup, my dress draped across a chair in the bedroom. I would never wear it again. Now it felt jinxed. I'd changed into a pair of shorts and a tank top. My stomach grumbled, reminding me that I'd not had dinner. I should have been hungry...but the mawing sensation in my belly didn't make me want to eat. It was too hot. My skin felt clammy, sticky. I hadn't smoked in over a year but now I wished I could have a cigarette. I longed for the illicit pull of the tobacco. I longed to forget.

How could he forget? How could I be so easy to forget? He used to remember everything. Every little detail of my life, memorizing it like it held some hidden meaning. He used to tell me he wanted to know everything about me. He'd remember things I'd forgotten. Now it felt like he'd forgotten all the important bits. Maybe he didn't want to remember.

For the first time in a long time, I found myself thinking about Niklas. He was remarried now. I'd been right all along...he remarried his ex-wife. Sometimes he called me, checking in, he'd say. Often bringing news of Jesper, whom I spoke to often, who came to visit once or twice a month. Occasionally, Niklas would tell me about Siri, about her latest boyfriend or how she was still running wild. We'd fall into an easy pattern and then suddenly he'd remember he couldn't call me like this too often; we weren't simply old friends. He never asked about Mads.

All those years I'd spent with Niklas...and then Mads had come along and opened my eyes to something new. I'd already been on a path of walking away without even realizing it. Was that what was happening now? Were Mads and I falling apart..? Was he traveling on that path now, longing for something—or someone—new?

* * *

When he came home, the summer night sky was finally dark. I was sitting on the balcony, trying to avoid going into the kitchen and snatching my emergency pack of cigarettes from its hiding place in the freezer. I hadn't smoked since I'd found out I was pregnant with Freya. I'd told myself I would quit now. I wanted to be a good role model for my daughters. I didn't want them to make the same stupid mistakes in life that I'd made. But the urge to smoke, to pour another glass of wine and blot out how humiliating it had been to sit there, waiting for him when he was enthralled in the company of another woman... maybe I was jumping the gun. But it niggled at me. We'd cheated...we'd been the ones who had the affair. What was stopping him from having another affair? He said he loved me...but now...well, now I wasn't so sure.

Below, the main door to our communal garden creaked open, then closed. Mads appeared but didn't look up. His footfalls echoed on the flagstones. I nearly called out to him but thought better of it. Instead, I left the balcony and walked through the apartment into the living room. I shivered a little. The air had cooled off now that the sun had finally set.

Mads opened the door and stepped in without seeing me. He pushed the door shut and then set his keys on the battered console table we used as a catch-all for everything...keys...bus tickets...magazines that needed to be recycled. He cursed under his breath...then he finally looked up and saw me standing there, arms crossed, waiting for him.

"Laney, I didn't mean for tonight to go this way." His jaw twitched. He ran his fingers over his lips. Had she kissed him? "I'm so sorry..."

I heard the guilt in his voice. He didn't approach me. Not at first. And the distance between us was like standing on opposite shores of Øresund Strait. I wanted to go to him, but I was afraid I'd lash out. I balled my hands into fists and kept them tucked under my crossed arms.

"Was that the infamous Benny...? The one all your shopmates are drooling over?"

He nodded. He kept his eyes trained on the white-washed oak floor.

His silence, like an admission of misdoings, crept up on me and nipped away at the calm veneer I was struggling to maintain. I didn't want to shout, not when the girls were sleeping. I didn't want them to hear us fighting again. I swallowed the bitterness rising in my throat. I kept telling myself I could do this—confront him without screaming. My mother had been the master of quiet force. Even at the worst of times, she never turned into one of those women who screamed and cried and caused scenes. Even when my father was intentionally pushing her buttons...she'd kept it together. I wanted my mother now. I wanted her here beside me, her hand on my shoulder as she assured me everything would be alright. That I would survive this. That I could live without him.

"You didn't tell me she looked like a fucking pinup model."

He tensed and shoved his hands in his pockets. Still he didn't say anything.

"Why did you even bother to suggest we go out and celebrate our anniversary?"

"I wanted us to have a special evening..."

"Oh, it was special alright. I sat there for an hour waiting for you. I felt like such a fool sitting there. And all while you were so consumed by Benny's fascinating... conversation. Or was it her breasts you were more interested in?"

Now he finally looked up. He opened his mouth to speak, then frowned. "There's nothing going on between me and Benny."

"Your body language—when I saw you together—said the opposite. You were staring at her breasts, Mads. You were looking at her like you wanted to fuck her right there on the table!"

"I don't want Benny! Fucking hell, Laney, you know I don't want anyone else!"

"I don't know *anything* anymore. I feel like I don't know *you* anymore." Saying it hurt. I could feel the pressure building inside me again. I didn't want to argue...I didn't want this at all, but the skin on my chest burned and tightened. I dropped my arms to my sides and bit down on my lip. The sharp thrust of pain distracted me enough to keep the worst of my anger at bay. *Don't shout, Laney, don't wake the girls...don't let them hear you.* "All I wanted tonight was a date night with you...I wanted us to feel like we were still connected. We could have done anything. I just wanted to be with you...and you forgot all about me! You didn't even answer my texts."

"I didn't hear my phone..."

"You could have called me, Mads! Why didn't you call me? Why did you..."

"I said I was sorry, Laney. As soon as we got the news, I wanted to call you and tell you, but then everything just got so hectic—and then the couriers showed up with the food..."

"If you could text me and say you'd be there in fifteen minutes, you could have called me and said there was a change of plans."

"Why can't you try to be happy for me? I'm finally at that point professionally where I wanted to be. This hotel project is what will cement my career."

I didn't want to hear this again. He was too blind to me now. I needed to be away from him but the only place I could escape to was our bedroom. This time he followed me. He said my name but I wouldn't turn, wouldn't look at him. Once we were in the room, he closed the door and said, "Don't pick a fight, Laney...haven't we had enough fights?"

"You just don't get it, do you?" I shrugged his hand off my shoulder. "Did you even once think about me? Think about the fact that you told me to go to that restaurant and wait for you...told me you wanted to make tonight about us getting back on track again..."

And that's when I saw it. The faint smudge of red on his neck...on the side of his face. It wasn't my shade of lipstick. We hadn't even kissed today.

"Did she kiss you?" I demanded. "Did you *let* her kiss you?"

"No...not on the mouth."

"Oh, but your neck was fine and dandy?"

"She was congratulating me—"

"She could've done that without kissing you!"

"Laney..."

"No. Get out of this room. You can't sleep here tonight. Go...go sleep in the guest room. Go sleep anywhere. But you can't sleep in here with me. I don't want you anywhere near me right now."

"We need to talk about this—"

"If I scroll through your phone, am I going to find any messages from her?"

"I haven't done anything wrong, Laney."

"No, but I'll bet you want to, though." My entire body went tight. Every part of me ached with rage that I was just barely holding in. "Is she going to Milan as well?"

He nodded. "So are Jonas, Morten, Ibrahim and Willem."

"Who are Ibrahim and Willem?"

"The other interns."

"Funny how they never come up in conversation as much as Benny has."

"You're overreacting."

"Are you attracted to her?"

He glanced away. I saw the tension building inside of him. Instead of answering me, he began undressing. Was he ever going to answer me?

I didn't want to cry anymore. I didn't want to think about Benny or what he might have done with her. I kept telling myself that maybe I was overreacting—maybe there was nothing going on between them, but the telling silence continued to fester. Mads went into our en suite bathroom. As soon as I heard the shower sputter on, I ended up following him. He was already in the shower stall, his back to me as the water streamed down his body. I watched as he rinsed off a day's worth of sweat...maybe even another woman's scent...from his skin. But standing there watching him...I hated that I still wanted him. I still wanted him to want me and only me. And I knew that tonight might be the last time I could have him to myself. Maybe it was already too late. I was trembling, still unable to stop this unsettled feeling inside me. And when he finally turned off the shower and reached for his towel, I ran my hands along his hips and pulled him close. He turned and the tight expression on his face nearly sent me away. I steeled myself. He exhaled slowly and leaned into me. He captured my lips with his, kissing me tenderly at first, his lips grazing mine, the tip of his tongue gently urging me to let him in. I squeezed my eyes shut and let my arms tighten around him. For a little while the rising heat between us was enough to make me forget. I let him peel away my camisole, let him push down my shorts. I kicked them aside. My body was coming alive for him even while my doubts were whispering to me, "This won't help..."

But I wanted him, wanted him to fuck me until I could stop feeling so empty inside. I wanted him to claim me, to make me his again. And as he lifted me, pressed me against the wall and I hooked my legs around him, I opened my eyes again and tried to remember every moment of this. He plunged into me and, once we were joined, a tiny ball of heat flamed inside me. "It's been too long..." he gasped in my ear. I tried to stay focused; I just wanted to feel how he throbbed inside me, remember each sensation of his chest against mine, his hands gripping my ass, my hips... the damp tile wall pressing into my back...With each thrust, with each moan, I told myself, "Remember this...remember how good it feels..." And I cried out as he touched me, deep inside, rubbing the right spot, sending waves of liquid heat through my veins, and still I wanted more.

He carried me into the bedroom, still buried deep inside me, still hard and ready for me...we fell onto the bed and he picked up the pace, pinning my hands over my head, keeping his eyes trained on me... I begged him to fuck me, forgetting that we were not alone in the apartment, that at any moment we might be interrupted, forgetting the balcony door was open and our neighbors could probably hear each squeak of the mattress, each creak of the bed frame and our ragged breaths, and Mads... moaning my name again and again. He fucked me...made me come once...and then again...until my body was sore, until he was finally satisfied. When he came, his body shuddered against mine, I writhed under him, wanting just a little more before the fog returned. He rolled off me, breathing heavily and reaching out to stroke my thigh.

"It's just you, Laney..." he said softly. He ran his fingertips along my thigh.

But I'd made up my mind already.

And I still wasn't sure I believed him.

CHAPTER FOUR: Mads

Is This the End?

She was on my mind all day. I'd be fine at first and then I'd remember the disappointment and simmering anger etched on her face when she walked into the workshop, when she saw me with Benny, and it would all come back. The argument, the sudden change of mood when she came to me in the bathroom. I thought maybe this was our first step to righting what was wrong...but when we went to bed, she didn't stay close to me and she inched away when I tried to bridge the gap. I needed to make this up to her. I couldn't fix this with sex. No matter how good it felt to be inside her again, to hear her moaning my name, to sense her every reaction to even the slightest move... we still weren't whole.

Jonas and Morten pretended not to notice my lack of focus. They talked around me, went to Anton with questions, and let me drown myself in sketching new ideas that didn't quite feel right. Even Benny kept her distance. She stayed on the other side of the workshop with

Ibrahim and Willem, assembling the credenza Anoushka had ordered. Had Anton warned her off? He'd greeted me with a gruff "*hej*" when I arrived but little else, which was unusual for him. Even at lunchtime he went off on his own instead of suggesting we go to Meyer's Deli or our usual café for coffee and *smørrebrød.* Maybe this was a good thing. I wasn't in the mood to talk to him or anyone else.

All I could think about was talking to Laney, hearing her voice and connecting with her again. I wasn't getting anything done, so I told Jonas and Morten I was going home, I had something I needed to do. They both nodded and sent regards to Laney. I bumped into Anton as I got to the corner.

"Where are you going?" he squinted at me. "I was just heading back...wanted to talk to you about something."

"I need to go home." My stomach growled. Maybe I could take Laney and the girls out to lunch. Maybe we could just sit in the garden and talk while the girls played together. "I need to talk to Laney."

"I was going to ask you about that, actually." Anton lit a cigarette and took a long drag. "We thought Sasha was spending the night...and then she showed up in a cab."

"I screwed everything up." I admitted. "Nothing went the way it should have..."

"You shouldn't have stayed last night." Anton frowned. He scratched his jaw and glanced over my shoulder. "I saw her when she came. And I saw why she left so quickly. You can't...fucking hell, Mads, she'd do anything for you and you fucking forgot you had a date with her?"

"I already feel like shit."

"You should. You should be on your knees begging her to forgive you." He scowled at me, then he nodded towards the workshop. "And we shouldn't keep Benny on. I don't think it's a good idea. Not for any of us."

"We can't fire her if she hasn't done anything wrong."

"You think Laney's going to forgive you when Benny's making a play for you?"

"Benny's not making a play for me."

Anton groaned. "You're blind then. Everyone else sees it."

"As long as she does her job, we can't fire her."

"Then I'm assigning her to work with Jonas and then either Ibrahim or Willem can work with you."

"I don't care right now...I just need to go home."

"Go. But think about what I said. I've known Laney a helluva long time. And I know she's not in a good place right now."

I waited at the door. Normally Liv came running to meet me, but today only silence and a strange stillness filled the apartment. I called out to Laney, but there was no reply. I'd grown so accustomed to Liv and Freya's excited outbursts that coming home to a quiet apartment was unnerving. I went from room to room but the apartment was empty.

The beds were all neatly made; the girls' toys were in their woven baskets. In our bedroom, the scene was much the same. Every room was empty. I checked my phone—no missed calls, no messages. I tried to remember where Laney usually took the girls during the day. Maybe she'd taken them to the aquarium. Liv loved going there and Freya always got so excited about the penguin and sea otters. When the weather was nice, she sometimes took the girls to visit my grandmother and then to the beach.

The apartment felt sterile without them. Where was the clutter Liv managed to produce no matter where she went? I missed Freya's excited shrieks and her chubby form wriggling and scooting across the floor. She was growing so fast. Soon she'd be walking...she was already trying to pull herself up. And her curiosity astounded me. If I was holding her and talking at the same time, she would stare at my mouth and try to move her lips the same way. Sometimes she'd cover my mouth with her fingers and giggle when I made funny noises against her palms. Often when I came home late, I'd go into the girls' room and fetch a sleeping Freya from her crib and bring her into the bedroom with Laney and me. I liked having her there with us, even though Laney said I was spoiling her. I liked the tiny noises she made when she slept, and how she inevitably ended up nestled against my chest, sucking one thumb as she drifted back into dreamland. Liv would eventually wander in, dragging her fox behind her, and scramble onto the bed. She'd whisper "*hej, papa...*" as she found her spot. Her wild halo of curls always made me smile. And when the four of us were in this little cocoon of sleep, all the problems that popped up during the day seemed to vanish.

I wanted that security, that sense of calm, now.

In my mind, I'd pictured coming home and finding Laney alone in the kitchen or maybe the bedroom. I'd planned it all out—the girls would be taking their after-lunch nap, Laney would be having some "me" time. And I'd show up, make up for being such a clueless asshole and we'd talk, maybe we'd make love again. And she'd forgive me. And I would be better. I would listen to her. I would help more. It sounded so simple. I knew Laney was not going to forgive me so easily. But I at least wanted a chance to show her that I loved her, that I wanted her to be happy.

I left several text messages for her, but she never answered. I hung around the apartment for another hour, hoping they'd return from their outing, then I went back to the workshop. The project lead for the hotel group was coming in for a meeting. Before I left the apartment, I wrote a note to Laney, told her I loved her and asked her to call me. In a way, this was better than nothing.
I would see her soon.

I would set things right again.

The meeting took longer than I'd expected. They always did. The hotel group was anxious to get started—but cautious in the design route they wanted to take. Most of their hotels had a very standard boutique hotel feel to them. Lots of dark wood, lots of beige walls that they kept calling warm, comforting neutrals. Jonas and I had spent several months coming up with ideas that would stray from this pattern. We wanted to work with teak, walnut and oak. We knew they liked our Hans Wegner–inspired chairs and side tables, so we'd focused on creating furniture designs that reflected the Danish Modern aesthetic without veering into a too-dated or retro feel. But the project lead was one of those too cool for you guys who wore a suit with slicked-back hair and a smirk. His name was Ole Biers, and he behaved as though Jonas and I were little boys who needed to be coddled.

"We're expecting something spectacular," he said at the end of the meeting. He flapped his right hand as though he were shooing away an annoying pigeon. "We need to wow the masses."

Jonas and I gave him a side eye. He'd been blathering on in similar platitudes throughout the meeting, wanting to completely change the very designs the owners had loved. We should have been prepared for this. There was always that client who swore they loved your work and then wanted to strip away everything they claimed to adore until there was nothing left but a generic shell. Once he was gone, Jonas jumped up and down, stomping his feet on the floor like a frustrated child having a temper tantrum. I rolled up the designs and cleared our hastily drawn revisions and coffee cups from the table.

"Shit, I hate that man!" Jonas banged his fists on the tabletop and grimaced. "He is like...pond scum! He doesn't know anything!"

"He's the one with the check," I reminded him. Even if we were doing well, we needed big clients like the hotel group if we wanted to keep a good reputation. But I agreed with Jonas. People like Ole...for them furniture and design was all about status. They didn't see the beauty in a perfectly honed piece of wood. They looked at what we created and only wondered how much it would be worth in the future or who would it impress. But he helped us pay the bills, so we couldn't always say no just because we didn't like the client.

"Yeah, well, next time let's make sure we bid on projects that don't involve assholes like him."

"Hindsight, Jonas, hindsight." I grinned and shook my head. It was late enough in the afternoon that the summer heat was building. The back of my T-shirt was damp with sweat. My skin felt hot and sticky... It would be good to go home and take a shower, change into a clean shirt and shorts.

I strode through the workshop to the back office. Anton was on the phone when I walked in. He nodded at me then lowered his voice. It must have been Ingrid on the other line. I grabbed my phone from the desk. One missed call—finally, it was Laney. But when I listened to the message—everything drained from me.

Hi, it's me....I can't be with you right now... I need a break. From you. From our life. I don't think you understand how difficult it's been. I feel like you don't see me, you don't care. I'm at home all day taking care of our daughters and you don't come home when you say you will. I'm drowning, Mads. I am drowning. I am hanging on by a thread and the only thing keeping me from sinking too far...it's Liv and Freya. I love them so much... I don't want them to ever feel like this. I don't want them to live with parents who maybe don't love or like each other. I don't know what's going wrong with me...with us. I love you, Mads, but I can't take this anymore...feeling like I am the only one keeping our life together, like I am the only one in our marriage. You said your work would never come before your family but it does...time after time. Jeg elsker deg so højt, Mads...but yesterday was the last straw. I'm so fucking tired of this...and you don't get it, you think your dream is more important than our family. I need you. I keep telling you this. I can't do this—raise our girls, keep us together, everything—on my own. So I'm going to figure out what I want. The girls and I...we need some peace.

I just remember saying "no"... It was the only word that was going through my head. No. And then this whooshing sensation, like the floor dropped from under me. Then...I don't know. . This... fury took over. Every ounce of reserve disappeared and all I could see was this life, my life, crumbling. I'd lost her. I'd let her go...I thought...I thought last night we'd reconnected. I thought it was a prelude to something better for us.

Damn it, Laney...no...just...no...

* * *

All night I tried to call her but my calls went to voicemail. Each time the message I left was the same: "Laney, please, where are you? I love you. Please, call me, come home..."

I couldn't stay at the workshop. I didn't want to go home. How could I stand it when she was gone? When my girls were gone? But where could I go? If I went to Henrik, Eddy would give me such a tongue-lashing that I would feel even worse. If I went to *farmor*, she would wonder why Laney and the girls were not with me. I ended up calling Adam. We hadn't spent much time together lately—there were still traces of resentment on both sides from Trine's attitude towards Laney. She still thought Laney was no good for me, even after all this time. She still thought our marriage was a bad idea. Yet she adored Liv and Freya and would shower them with so much affection. Laney had always tolerated it. She figured it was better that Trine liked our children rather than concentrating on us, but she didn't trust Trine with them. But when I called Adam, he said he couldn't meet me.

"I've got a family dinner," he said. "Trine will kill me if I try to get out of it."

"Maybe tomorrow then."

But I didn't think he'd call back. And I didn't tell him what happened.

Anton was still hanging around. I knew he wanted to talk to me, but I tried to put him off. I didn't want to hear any "I told you so's—even if I deserved it. He hovered, though, scratching his head, rapping his knuckles on the doorframe, whistling off tune.

And he wouldn't let me get away with avoiding him.

"I know where she is," he said with no preamble. "She told Ingrid."

"You know...?"

He nodded. "She called Ingrid this morning—but Ingrid didn't tell me until a few minutes ago."

"Where is she?""

"She's on a plane."

"Don't be so fucking cryptic, just tell me where my wife is."

"She's on a plane. She's on her way to America."

"Anton, she left me." Saying it still didn't take away the awful reality of it. Laney walked away from me. We said we'd never do it... she always told me she didn't want to be in the same situation her mother had been in. That she would fight for us. But maybe she'd been fighting all along and I'd missed the signs.

"I know."

"She left me..."

"It's not too late, Mads. Not if you really want her back. But you have to give her this time she needs."

"I don't want to be away from her—"

"You've been away from her for months." He scoffed. "You've been here sometimes until midnight instead of going home. You've been here trying to convince everyone how fucking great we are instead of going home to your wife."

"*Fanden*, Anton, you know how many clients we've had. I couldn't just leave when everyone else was working their asses off to meet deadlines."

"No one would have faulted you for going home and spending some time with Laney and the girls. They would've understood." Anton shrugged. "I told Morten and Jonas about how Laney was feeling...how she was having a difficult time after the pregnancy. That's why they were working late all the time. I tried to get you to go home, but you wouldn't."

"They knew?"

He nodded and then shrugged again. "I tried to tell you."

"I thought they were staying because we were behind schedule." I rubbed the bridge of my nose, hoping it would ease away the dull pain inside me. "I only stayed because I thought they needed my help..."

"I wish you'd listened, Mads. I've been trying to tell you for months that Laney was not doing so well. I thought you'd see it. I thought you'd take care of her...like you did when Liv was born. You were so devoted to her—Ingrid is furious with you right now, I'm trying not to be, but damn, it's hard."

"How am I supposed to go home now? I can't be there without her..."

"Yes, you can. Give her a month. Give her some time to heal and then you go to her."

"Where is she going...?"

"America."

"Where, though?"

"She'll call you, Mads. She just needs some time."

"I want to speak to her, though—"

"She's on a goddamned plane, you won't be able to talk to her anyway."

Sinking, sinking. My wife leaves me, my friend and his wife know. And all I knew was that she needed to be away from me. That I was the reason she no longer felt she could hold on.

Once Anton left, I knew I couldn't hang around any longer. I went through the workshop, making sure all the machines were turned off, locking everything that needed to be locked.

Everyone else had gone home or headed out to enjoy the long summer night.

I tried to shut it all out as I walked home.

Back to the silence.

Back to being reminded that I'd driven her away.

CHAPTER FIVE: Laney

I Fall Apart

I don't know how I made it through the flight without falling apart. I kept telling myself to keep it together, keep the girls happy and entertained, make them think this is an adventure, make them think Daddy would join us in a few days...maybe a few weeks. I didn't even think when I was packing our bags. I just grabbed whatever was clean.

But now we were somewhere over the north Atlantic. Freya was drooling on my shoulder. Liv was sleeping in the seat next to mine. The flight attendants kept coming over to coo over my little girls and tell me how precious they were. I guess the other passengers were happy they were so calm. Hell, I was, too. I wasn't sure what to expect. I'd flown with Liv to the US when she was a baby and the flight was a nightmare—too much turbulence, Liv had colic and cried for close to two hours, Mads was airsick. By the time we arrived in New York, my nerves were frayed. And I said I would never fly with a baby again.

I still couldn't believe I'd done it. I'd left him.

Thinking about him...about how he'd touched me, how he'd reclaimed me last night...still sent electric shivers through me. But...then a flash of what had led to it was enough to dull the longing. The lipstick smudge...his nonchalance... our anniversary date in shambles, the argument. As if she sensed it too, Freya stirred and let out a tiny cry. I rocked her and murmured in her ear. She soon settled, but I wondered how long I would be able to soothe her so easily.

One of the attendants knelt beside me. "We found a baby cot for you," she said. "In case you want to put her down for a nap."

I thanked her and stood aside while she set it up on the floor in front of Liv's seat. She took the blanket I'd brought with me and lined the cot with it; she even found Mr. Penguin and set him there. We settled Freya into the cot and then swaddled her with the blanket.

"Is this her first flight?" the attendant asked.

"Yes...first flight, first vacation without her father, too."

"Just a trip for the girls, then."

I nodded. It was mostly true.

"The three of you will have a wonderful time together, I'm sure." She patted my shoulder. "Just let me know if you need anything else."

I thanked her and watched as she returned to the galley. Liv had shifted in her seat. Her blanket had slid down to her lap. I readjusted it and wondered if she understood what was happening. Would she forgive me if things never improved, if the only way to getting back to me was to leave Mads for good?

My sleeping girls dreamed on, probably dreaming of foxes and penguins. It was a nicer dream than the reality of being without their father.

My aunt met us at Miami International Airport with all the fanfare of visiting dignitaries. In one hand, she was waving a Danish flag and an American flag; in the other she was holding a handwritten sign emblazoned with "Halliwell-Rasmussen Family." Any other day, I would have rolled my eyes at such a sight but today it made me cry. Though she looked nothing like my mother, Aunt Cecily was the closest thing I had to a mother after my own mother lost her battle with breast cancer. Aunt Cecily was whom Liv called "gramma" — as close as she managed to get to "grandmother" or "grandmom." Even now, a still groggy Liv was squealing with delight at seeing Cecily waving flags for her. She let go of my hand and ran over to her, throwing herself into my aunt's waiting arms and giggling as she was welcomed with hugs and kisses. Freya was more cautious. The last time my aunt had been in Copenhagen, Freya was just a few days old. She'd only seen pictures of her. "Don't worry," I told my more reserved daughter as we pushed our luggage trolley over to where my aunt was waiting. "This is your gramma, and she loves you so very much."

With Liv now in her arms and commandeering the flags, my aunt gave me a fierce hug and then she patted Freya's cheeks and said, "You are a little doll, aren't you? Looking exactly like your mother when she was a tiny one!" Freya seemed to accept this. She reached out for Cecily, wanting now to be held by someone besides me.

"Thank you for letting us come at such short notice." We were walking now towards the exit for short-term parking. "I really appreciate this, Cecily."

My aunt shushed me and pressed a kiss to my cheek. "Nonsense, my dear. You needed me, and I am here for you. Now let's get these two cuties to the car. You must be exhausted after that flight."

I was. I could only imagine how I looked. I was certain I had bags under my eyes, Freya's drool stains on the shoulder of my shirt. Long flights always made me crave a shower. Breathing in all that recycled air, being too close to so many other people for such a long period of time... That's all I wanted...to take a shower, to wash away everything awful and to feel whole again.

"Does Mads know you're here?"

"Not yet, no."

"I want you to call him once we get the little ones settled and tell him where you are." We were outside now. The oppressive heat and humidity slapped me in the face and made me gasp.

"Slowly, sweetie..." My aunt made me stop. "Just breathe in and out slowly. Let your lungs get used to it."

"I always forget..."

"I know, my darling. You've been away from this sort of heat for a very long time."

"Am I doing the right thing?"

We started walking again. Liv was chattering, telling Cecily about her fox and how Bobbi Fox was going to love our adventure. Freya was giggling and taking in all the sights and sounds. My aunt didn't answer me until we'd found her car and loaded all of our bags into the trunk.

"I don't know, Laney. But you look like you needed a break, and that's exactly what I am going to make sure you get."

My aunt came prepared. She'd made sure there were two car seats—one for Liv and one for Freya. In my haste to make an escape, I'd not even thought about it. Once we strapped the girls in, we headed off towards my aunt's new home. I'd never pictured my aunt as a snowbird. For me, she was the quintessential New Yorker. But even when Eddy and I were teenagers, we used to wonder if Aunt Cecily was really meant to be someplace else. She was practicing yoga before celebrities made it trendy. She was a health-food nut who gave us green smoothies with our breakfast every morning.

Around ten years ago, she grew tired of New York's snow chaos after one blizzard too many. She sold the brownstone Eddy grew up in and where I'd lived once my mother was gone, and moved to Florida. At first she lived in Miami, but then she decided the people there were just as crazy as in New York and so she headed north along the Atlantic coastline until she found the perfect four-bedroom bungalow in Juno Beach. The crazy thing was that she looked so relaxed, so happy—even in the face of her wayward niece showing up with two toddlers—that it made me wonder what was her secret. Was it the Florida air? Was it the warmth 365 days a year? My sixty-nine-year old aunt looked younger and more harmonic than most people my age.

I was still thinking about how I wished I could be more like her when she asked me if I'd thought about what I was going to do now that I was here.

"No, not really," I admitted. We passed palm tree after palm tree. Sometimes I glimpsed the Atlantic Ocean and wondered when I would be able to take a dip and lose myself for a while. I glanced back at Liv and Freya. They'd fallen asleep again. I was pretty sure I would pay for this later but at least they were calm.

"It hasn't been easy—and I didn't expect it to be. I just didn't think he would leave me in the lurch."

"My darling, what is going on with you and that handsome husband of yours? When I was there in January, I never saw a more devoted man."

"I don't know what happened. One day he was there all the time, helping, being the kind of father I always knew he would be...and then he just...stopped."

"Did you try to speak to him about it?"

I nodded. "He doesn't understand, though. He thinks that I don't need his help. He thinks I manage to do everything on my own. And I don't."

"Well, I have to say, I've never seen you look so worn out, even when the two of you were having to go back and forth to the hospital for Liv."

"I'm fine..."

"If you were fine, you wouldn't have left your husband."

"I haven't left him."

"Well, you're here, he's there and he hasn't got a clue where you are. Sounds like you left him."

Put like that, there was no way to pretend I had not done so. I turned my face away, kept my eyes trained on the line of trees and concrete barriers we passed. It was probably around one in the morning in Copenhagen. Mads would be going crazy...wondering where we were. He'd probably tried to track me down through Eddy and Ingrid.

"We'll get you sorted out in the morning," my aunt said wistfully. She patted my knee then turned on the car stereo. One of her meditation podcasts filled the car with clinking cymbals and the sound of the wind.

It was closing in on dinnertime when we arrived. My aunt helped us get situated. She took the girls to show them the room where they would sleep. Liv asked if her daddy would sleep there too. My aunt didn't miss a beat. "When he arrives, he can sleep here too." This seemed to please Liv enough that she didn't ask more questions, but every now and then she'd flicker her eyes toward me and the confused look I saw made me feel ashamed for leaving the way I did.

I slept fitfully. Twice I reached for Mads, my body craving his firmness and his heat, only to remember too late that he was not with me. At some point, Liv crawled into bed with me. She croaked a very hoarse "Mommy" as she stroked my cheek. "I'm here," I whispered. I wasn't sure what time it was. The sky was still dark, but I could hear seagulls so it must have been close to sunrise.

"Mommy's here..."

Her springy curls tickled my neck as she shifted in the unfamiliar bed. "The bed smells funny here," she said in Danish. "It smells like candy..."

"It's the fabric softener," I murmured to her. "Gramma uses a different one from us."

"Why?"

"Because they don't sell the one we like here," I told her. "I'll look for another brand when we go to the store and then we can wash your sheets."

"Okay...I don't think Papa will like candy sheets."

"No, probably not."

"When is Papa coming?"

"Soon..." I pressed a kiss to the top of her head. She still smelled warm and sleepy. Maybe she would fall asleep again...I wasn't ready to talk about Mads yet. I hadn't called him last night, even though I'd promised Aunt Cecily I would. His voice...even now when I was furious with him...I knew it would make me melt. The roughness of it, the way he could say my name and it sent waves of lust through me, no...it was better not to call him yet. I needed a clear head to speak with him. But Liv...she was used to speaking to him every day, seeing him every day. She would want to talk to her father. I couldn't isolate the kids from him. No matter how upset I was, I couldn't keep our children from him forever. Sooner or later...he would demand to see them, even if he gave up on me.

"But when, Mommy?"

"Soon...he'll come soon." But for now, no matter how much my body wanted Mads's, my mind was telling me we needed a break. And even if it meant telling a white lie to my daughter, I needed peace of mind. I loved him...maybe I loved him too much.

But I couldn't be with him.

Not right now.

The next morning, Aunt Cecily treated us to a "proper" American breakfast of pancakes, scrambled eggs, fried apples and bacon. Both Liv and Freya were mystified—our version of American breakfast was usually just scrambled eggs and bacon, maybe some bagels if we had time to pick any up from Torvnehallerne. At first, Liv picked at her fried apples, but Cecily convinced her to taste a tiny bit.

Liv clapped excitedly. "Mommy, *det smager ligesom jul!*"

I smiled at her. "It does, doesn't it?" Then I said to Cecily, "She says it tastes like Christmas—so that's a good thing."

Freya was in the highchair beside me, using a Winnie-the-Pooh toddler spoon to feed herself. I watched as she managed to get fried apples in her hair, on her nose...sometimes in her mouth. The sides of my mouth twitched into a smile. I asked her if she wanted more apples. She nodded and declared them "nam-nam"—Freya's favorite way of saying "delicious". Anything nam-nam was good—she could be such a fussy eater sometimes.

My aunt was watching the whole exchange. I wondered if she was analyzing it. "Can Liv understand English?"

"Mostly," I said. "So if you want to ask me something...personal, maybe we should wait."

Cecily nodded. "We need to fix you, Laney. But we'll talk about that when little ears aren't listening."

Once we'd eaten, and the girls were bathed and dressed, we took them for a walk—Liv in her stroller, Freya in the Baby Björn backpack that Mads usually used. The tree-lined street Aunt Cecily lived on was in a neighborhood called Dido Gardens. It was not directly on the beach, but it only took a few minutes to walk there and when Liv saw the long expanse of beach and then the glittering ocean, she jumped up and down in her stroller and called out to me, "Mommy, Mommy! *Havet*!"

"It's beautiful, isn't it?" The Atlantic Ocean glittered green in the morning sun. Freya, too, seemed charmed by it. Though I often took them to Amager Strand and Hellerup, they were not used to seeing a sea so vast.

Aunt Cecily pointed to a playground with a view of the beach. "Let's go there so the girls can work off a little of that jet lag."

At the playground, Liv was suddenly shy. She hovered, not wanting to approach the other children. I assured her it would be okay and walked her over to the swing set. Aunt Cecily was on the play center with Freya, taking her on the slide and having a blast. I asked Liv if she wanted to do that instead, but she shook her head no and began to cry.

I picked her up and held her tightly. My sweet Liv, so tired, so confused by hearing so much English around her when she was used to hearing more Danish...sleeping in a new house, not having her father around. It was all too much for her today.

With each sob, a piece of my will shattered. She was well and truly a daddy's girl. Even when Mads worked late he would find time for Liv. Everything we went through to bring her into the world...the nights we spent together at the hospital, learning to care for our prematurely born daughter, terrified she might not make it through her first months of life... If anyone had all of Mads's heart it was Liv. And for Liv, Mads was the sun, the moon, the stars. She might like cuddles from me, but she adored her father—broken promises and all. At home, her eyes followed him wherever he went. She trailed him, always ready to clamber into his lap, always finding pebbles or bits of paper to present to him as if they were the finest gifts. Sometimes I'd find them napping together on the sofa or their heads bent over drawings—Mads sketching new ideas for future projects, Liv scribbling family portraits or animals. And in the evenings, if Mads was home early, only he could tuck her in.

Freya and Aunt Cecily spent a few more minutes on the play center before they joined us on the bench.

"You know, it's not going to get any easier." Cecily unzipped the cooler bag we'd brought with us. She rummaged around inside it until she found Freya's sippy cup. "One of the hardest things you can do is be a single parent."

"I know... I'm not taking any of this lightly."

"I know you aren't, Laney... and I know you needed to come here. You look worn out...don't protest, I see it—there's no light in your eyes, you move like there is no fire in you anymore."

"I'll be fine—"

"Not if you don't take care of yourself."

"I don't have time to think about me."

"Of course you do. That's why you're here. Now, I think I know how to help you."

"I was hoping you'd have a solution," I admitted. My arms were numb from holding Liv for so long. I brushed her hair back from her forehead. She'd fallen asleep again, so I put her in the stroller and draped my shawl over it to keep the worst of the sun off her. She wasn't used to this strong sunlight and we'd forgotten sunscreen at my aunt's house.

"Well, I do. You need a babysitter, to start with."

"And you've got one?"

"I do. My neighbor's oldest daughter, Peyton. I'll introduce you to her. She could come by, watch Liv so you could go out, meditate..."

"Meditate...? You know I don't do that..."

"Well, maybe you should. I think some meditation and yoga would help you... and it would help this little one too." Cecily tickled Freya's belly. My youngest daughter kicked out her chubby legs and smiled up at her surrogate grandmother. "I know you love her...but you don't seem as bonded with her as you should be. I can see it. And you don't want this sweet little girl growing up thinking her mother does not love her."

"I do love her—"

"Laney, I know you do, but you've had these blues so long you don't see that your love for her pales in comparison to how you are with Liv."

There it was. My dirty little secret out in the open. I covered my mouth with my hand... all the times I'd felt like I was going through the motions with Freya when I should have been feeling overwhelmed with love for her.

On rare days I held her and wondered if she was really mine, this slippery, wriggly little girl who seemed to want only me, even when I sometimes wanted nothing more than to sleep. Those days when I felt numb, when I had to fake enthusiasm for the new things she could do...I knew it was these blues eating away at me.

"I don't know what do, Auntie."

"Tomorrow, you and Freya will come to the yoga studio with me. We have a Baby & Me yoga class. I think it'll be good for you. And for Freya."

The rest of the afternoon, my aunt's words of advice were still reeling through my mind. If she could see that my devotion to my youngest daughter wasn't as strong as it should be, how many other people were observant enough to notice it? Had Mads noticed it? Was this why he often went to her and showered her with affection before he even came to me? When Freya scrambled into my lap as I unpacked our suitcases, I made sure to give her more cuddles and kisses. She reached for my cheek and patted me. I smiled down at her. She had her father's eyes—surprisingly dark, flashing green and copper...I'd thought that Liv would have Mads's eyes, but her eyes were a golden-brown like mine. Freya even had the same splash of brown freckles across her nose as her father. Somehow I'd never noticed this until now, and it shamed me. How many other things had I missed because of this awful, awful fog?

My throat constricted—oh Christ, I was going to start crying. My eyes were already burning, my head throbbing. Freya blinked at me and sang "ma-ma-la-la" at me. Her tinkling voice made me smile and then laugh again. Tears were already sliding down my cheeks but it was this moment—so sweet and clear and the sort of moment I'd longed for with Freya, seeing her, holding her and loving her. I wanted more moments like this with her.

I didn't hear my aunt when she came into the room. She stood in the doorway, watching as Freya sang to me and I tickled my little one's tummy.

"So you'll come tomorrow?" Cecily asked.

"Yes." I rocked Freya as a well of giggles erupted from her. "We'll both come."

Later, after I'd bathed the girls, after I'd read to them and tucked them in, I closed the door to my bedroom, sat on the edge of my bed and turned on my phone for the first time since we'd arrived. My message inbox was full of text messages and voicemail from Mads. I read every message... *Laney, where are you? Laney, please call me... Laney, I love you, please, call me, tell me you are okay. Why did you leave? Why? Laney...why...I love you... I can't stand this. Why? Where are you...please...call me... I need to know you're okay...*

His voicemails too tore my heart to shreds. I heard the fear, the confusion, the pain in his voice. With each pause, each ragged breath, I pictured him tearing from room to room looking for us. "...I know I screwed up,

Laney. I thought... I thought... Tell me where you are. I'll come, just tell me."

His voice crept along my spine, sparking every nerve fiber in me. It hurt to be with him...it hurt even more to be away from him. I listened to his messages again and again, unable to resist the pull. He'd sobbed as if I'd ripped his heart from his chest. "I don't know how to live without you, Laney...just, please, tell me where you are."

That evening I dared to do what my aunt said I ought to do. I called Mads, knowing that it was the middle of the night in Denmark. His phone rang twice before it went to his voicemail. Once his outgoing message finished playing, I cleared my throat and said, "Hi...it's me. The girls and I are okay. But...you can't come here. Not yet."

And then I hung up, and everything inside me fell apart.

CHAPTER SIX: Mads

The Truth Hurts

I couldn't sleep. The apartment was too still. Without the veil of background noises compliments of Laney, Liv and Freya, our home felt more like a mausoleum or a museum of what my life used to be like. I moved through the apartment like a ghost, trying not to see the gallery wall with all of our family photos—if I stopped, if I even glimpsed one of our wedding photos or Liv's first school picture from daycare, I fell apart. When I did manage to drift off, I dreamt she lay beside me, grazing her fingertips along the nape of my neck, pressing her lips to mine and whispering, "It's okay, baby. We'll get through this." Sometimes in the dreams she'd sling her legs over mine and we'd sit like that...imagining we were the only people in the world. Other times she'd kneel between my legs, undo my zipper and take me in her mouth, pulling and sucking me so gently I knew I was dreaming... and then she'd quicken the pace, graze her teeth against my shaft and suck so hard I felt like she was drawing my soul out of me. I'd wake in a cold sweat, my hand gripping my cock and her name sliding off my tongue. It took a few minutes to recover... I'd turn on my side, ready to say, "I had the most intense dream about you..." but there'd come no reply. Of course there wouldn't. She'd left me.

Today was no different. They'd been gone three days now. And I still didn't know where she was. I'd called Eddy but she refused to break Laney's confidence and said, "If you think hard enough, you'll figure it out. But I'm not going to just spell it out for you." Henrik wouldn't tell me either. I'd thought he'd want to put me out of my misery, but he was siding with Eddy. I guess I shouldn't have been surprised. Henrik's advice when it came to relationships was that you should always listen to your woman and always have her back. I used to tease him and say it sounds like the World According to Barry White, but without fail he'd shrug and say, "It works." Ingrid was no help either. Instead of telling me, she railed at me. She was so protective of Laney and I was glad she was. She proved time and again how much she cared about my wife. And now she was ready to stand between Laney and me to keep me from hurting Laney emotionally. How could I be angry when Ingrid was doing what I should have been doing from the start?

I tried to crack the password on her computer, but apparently I didn't know my wife well enough to figure it out. I sat at her desk—the desk I'd made for her—wracking my brain and trying to figure out what words would mean enough to her to be used as passwords. If I could figure it out, then maybe I'd find her itinerary and then I could go to her.

Last night, she finally called me back. I'd missed the call—it was still so humid at night and I'd given up with tossing and turning at 2AM to take a cold shower. When I came back in the bedroom, I saw her name and "*ubesvarede opkald*" on my phone display and screeched out a string of curses. I listened to her message; she was telling me to stay away...for now. She still wouldn't say where she was. I tried to call her back but my calls went straight to voicemail. She must have turned off her telephone. So now the only way I could communicate with her was by sending text messages and hoping she'd reply, waiting, and trying to figure out when she'd turn her phone on again.

Going to the workshop didn't feel like an option today. I needed to clear my head, needed to think straight, and I didn't think I'd get anything worthwhile done, not when I was so distracted. I called Jonas and told him I was taking a couple of days off. He was stoic about it. He knew everything and said, "We've got it covered, Mads. You do what you need to do, man."

I couldn't stay here in the apartment all day, and it had been a couple of weeks since I'd last visited my grandmother. Laney usually stepped in here. She visited Alma with the girls at least once a week, called her several times a week checking in and making sure the home help Henrik and I had arranged was taking good care of her. Another reason to feel guilty. Another way Laney made things easy for me, shouldering my responsibility when she had enough to do. I ended up riding my bike across Fredensbro and over to Norreport Station. I needed a break from the heat of the city, from my empty home...I needed to be near the sea again.

Taking the train to Humlebæk always felt like returning to my childhood. When my mother was still alive, when we were still living with my father, we always escaped to my grandmother's house on days when my mum would say the sea was calling. She and my grandmother would lock arms and walk barefoot along the beach while I ran ahead, oblivious to the turmoil my mother was dealing with. Even when Laney and I came out here together, it was much the same. She and my grandmother would walk together while I ran ahead with the kids, whooping and hollering with them, chasing seagulls as the waves lapped the shore. I didn't stop to look back unless Freya or Liv began to panic about the distance. They needed to see Laney, wave to her and make sure she hadn't suddenly vanished. But she was always there, waving back to them and calling out how much she loved them.

I lowered my head into my hands and swore. Maybe this was a bad idea. My grandmother's house wouldn't be neutral territory, devoid of any reminders of my wife and our life together. Farmor probably had more photos of us than we had ourselves. The train rumbled along the tracks, leaving the city behind and heading through the green, flat countryside. Denmark wasn't full of dramatic terrain but there was something beautiful in its rolling hills, but this too reminded me of Laney. The hills like the curves of her hips, her breasts... Someone once said it was a terrible sign of weakness to want your wife too much. I suppose I was weak, then. I loved every inch of her. I squandered her love but that didn't stop me from lusting for her, wanting to strip her naked and taste her. That night...when we finally made love again, the heat of her skin, her sweet, milky scent mingled with the soapy scent of my skin...how she gripped me, pulled me in. I was lost in her...lost in that feeling of rediscovering my wife. I thought we were forgiving one another.

When I raised my head again, the train was pulling into Humlebæk Station. I joined the other passengers filing off the train. That's when I saw him—my father, Benjamin Rasmussen, at the ticket machine. We had not seen one another in several weeks. Not since Laney had invited him over for a Sankt Hans barbecue.

"*Hej, far.*" I ducked my head at him. "Have you been to visit *farmor*?"

My father continued adding his coins to the machine methodically, counting out each coin without answering me. The same grim face he always wore except when he could see his granddaughters. At least he showed them the love and affection he never extended to me.

I waited. Once the machine printed his ticket, he peered at it, making certain it was correct. Now my father finally looked at me, giving me a once-over, as

Laney called it, before he said, "It's good to see you, Mads. I was going to come by your workshop today, but now you have saved me a trip into the city."

"You look good, *far*." His skin looked healthier and he'd gained some weight. Had he stopped drinking? I wanted to ask him, but even now our relationship was not like that.

Benjamin grunted dismissively. He wasn't one for small talk. "You should know. Laney and the little ones came to see me. Before she went to the airport."

"You saw her?"

"Yes, she wanted me to know she was going away for a while. She didn't want me to worry."

The irony of it was like a swift kick to the head. She didn't want my father to worry. She didn't even see my father that often, did she?

"You know, she brings the girls to visit me. Sometimes we meet at La Glace for cake and coffee." My father checked the clock, then shook his head. "She wasn't in a good way the last few times I saw her."

"She never told me you were meeting so often." I rubbed the back of my neck and stared down at the dusty station floor. "She never said..."

"She wasn't in a good way the last few times we met," my father said again. "I left messages on your phone, but you never returned my calls."

Benjamin gestured towards the opposite platform. I walked with him to the other side where the train back to Copenhagen would stop. We didn't speak as we walked down the steps and through the tunnel under the tracks to the other side. I let my father catch his breath from climbing the stairs. Years of heavy smoking had taken their toll on him. I still didn't understand how he climbed so many stairs to his apartment.

"Your wife...she's a good woman, Mads, and yet she is sad." Benjamin sniffed. "She told me once she felt like she was a bad mother...that she wasn't giving the children enough love..."

"She never told me this."

"No, well...you've been very busy."

"Did she tell you anything else?"

"She went to a doctor...some weeks ago. He told her she needed a break, perhaps a change of scenery and some help with the children. She was looking forward to your vacation. She thought it would help her find her way back to the way she used to be."

The more he said the more my skin burned with shame. Had I been so blind, so deaf to my wife? I stared off in the distance, not wanting to meet my father's calm, frank mien. Laney kept so many secrets. Or maybe I simply hadn't listened.

"How long did you know she was like this?" I finally managed to ask my father.

"Three months ago. I called you. I even stopped by your workshop but that intern of yours said you were busy with clients. I suppose she didn't tell you I was there."

I shook my head no. Or at least I didn't remember Benny mentioning it. Perhaps she had, but it was so long ago.

"At any rate, she said you were too busy..."

"I'm never too busy for my family—" but I cut myself short when the stoic expression on my father's face hardened. I glanced away. I couldn't keep lying to myself.

"You need to be careful, Mads. Your daughters, they adore you now. Just like you used to be about me. But if you don't change your ways, you'll end up as distanced from them...and your wife... as you and I have been for so long."

The train pulled into the station. My father shook my hand then boarded the train. I stood on the platform, watching as he moved through the train and found a seat. He lifted his hand in a wave, then turned away from the window. Further down the platform the signal sounded and the train departed, heading back to Copenhagen. I waited until the train disappeared from sight. My father knew my wife better than I did. My father—who'd been unable to deal with my mother and me or everyday life without numbing himself with alcohol—could keep himself sober for his granddaughters.

I wasn't sure how much time passed before I finally left the station. But as I walked to my grandmother's house, I tried to ignore the horrible irony of my situation. My father was closer to my family than I was. And Laney confided in him when she could not do so with me.

* * *

Farmor was in her garden when I arrived. She had her favorite spot—near the far end of the garden, under the protective canopy of the beech tree my grandfather planted when they first bought this house. Her home helper had set two chairs out, though only Alma sat there, her eyes closed and a smile curling the corners of her lips. *Farmor* looked happy, satisfied. I almost didn't want to disturb her, but I was pretty sure she'd already heard me come through the gate.

"So you've finally come," she said and squeezed my hand. "I wondered how long it would take before my grandson would stop working long enough to visit."

"I'm sorry, *farmor*, I know I should have come sooner." I nodded at the extra chair. "Was that for *far* or *farfar*?"

"It was for your grandfather, but he won't mind if you take it." Sometimes my grandmother behaved as though my grandfather were still very much alive. She said his ghost kept her company, humming the songs they remembered from their youth and reminding her of all the special moments they'd shared. "Sit, Mads...it's been too long since I last saw you."

"I know...it won't happen again."

"Don't turn into my prodigal grandson. And don't turn into your father. I love Benjamin dearly but the years he wasted...well, at least he is trying to get himself together for the sake of Liv and Freya."

I nodded. This was the lesson she'd tried to teach me all my life—to be the man my grandfather was, rather than the man my father was. My father had filled a void of insecurity and frustration with alcohol. He'd loved it more than he loved my mother and me.

"*Farmor*, did he tell you what's happened?" There was no point in trying to hide it from her. Sooner or later someone would tell her.

"Your father? Yes, yes. He told me that Laney is gone." My grandmother sighed and shook her head. "But I knew already. Laney called me to say goodbye. I'm sure she will come back. Or you will go and you will convince her to come back."

"I don't know where she is. She won't tell me."

"She went to her family."

"She doesn't have any family, *farmor*. Just me and the girls..."

"There is Eddy too," my grandmother surmised. "And of course there is Eddy's mother."

"I don't think she went there," I said. "Laney wouldn't go so far—"

"You've got to make things right, Mads. Don't let her slip through your fingers. Remember what you told me the first time you brought her here."

I nodded. I still remembered sitting in my grandmother's living room with Laney beside me, my heart practically bursting from all the love I felt for her, even then.

"Don't let your work...or anyone else...get in the way. Ever."

We sat for a long time, not speaking. I leaned forward, resting my arms on thighs and staring down at the grass. She'd said goodbye to everyone...except me.

"*Farmor*, did Laney tell you where she was going?"

"She did," Farmor said. "But I don't think I should betray her confidence. Not unless you plan on doing something about it."

"Will you tell me?"

"No, I don't think I will." Farmor let out a sigh and then patted my knee. "Laney will tell you in her own time. And really, she is the one who should tell you."

"I just want to know that she and the girls are okay."

"Don't you worry about that. She's in safe hands." My grandmother pushed herself to her feet. I jumped up, ready to help. She tutted at me. "I'm not an invalid, Mads."

"Have you spoken to her? Has she called you, *farmor*?"

But my grandmother didn't answer. She was walking along the edge of the garden, examining her rosebushes and tsk-tsking over the state of them. I knew how much she loved her garden and I needed a distraction. I spent the rest of the afternoon deadheading roses and pulling weeds while my grandmother reminisced about my grandfather and told me about my father's visit. I thought she'd change her mind and share Laney's whereabouts with me, but she was adamant. At least I knew for sure she was in America and she was with Eddy's mother. I couldn't remember where Eddy's mother lived, but I'd met Cecily twice. Aside from Eddy, and

Laney's father—whom we had no contact with—Cecily was Laney's only family. She took her in when Laney's mother died. Liv called her "gramma"—her version of grandmother. If Laney was with Cecily, then I knew I didn't have to worry. But that didn't stop me from missing her and wanting to go to her.

* * *

We didn't speak directly. I didn't know if Laney had her phone on all the time.

I left messages, she left messages. It went on like this for several days. She still would not tell me where she was.

"Why can't you just tell me?" I'd demanded so many times but the answer was always the same—silence. What made it worse was knowing that our friends knew—Anton, Ingrid, Henrik, Eddy—they all knew but none of them would break their promise to Laney. I should have been glad they loved her so much they were willing to keep her secrets, even from me. I asked her when I could speak to Liv, if we could at least have a Skype call so I could see the girls. At first she didn't reply. I waited. Re-sent the message. Several hours went by before she finally answered, "On Saturday, at 3PM your time, you can talk to the girls."

"Where are you? Please...tell me."

Her only reply was silence.

When Laney and I first moved in together, deep down I was afraid she would leave me. There was a part of me that anticipated her waking up one day and announcing she was going back to Niklas. Even when I knew she was happy with me. Even when we were so intense it often felt like no one else in the world existed... self-doubt had a way of picking me apart at the seams. If Niklas called, warning lights flashed. I'd go stony and silent as I waited for Laney to end the conversation and tell me the news. It never came. Sometimes I'd dream about her getting married to him and I'd wake up determined to convince her that I was the man for her. She sensed when these moments of insecurity rattled me. Sometimes she'd tell me little snippets of the bad times in their relationship...what went wrong, why she would never go back to him. Eventually I heard enough to accept that she was where she wanted to be.

Now I almost wished she'd gone to Stockholm with the girls. At least I'd know where to look for them. America was too big. I thought about calling Jesper. I knew he was in New York now. He'd moved there in January to work on his bachelor's degree. But I wasn't even sure if he was in New York City. Laney had only said "New York," and I'd been so preoccupied with helping Liv build a LEGO castle that it never occurred to me to ask if she meant the city or the state. Calling Jesper was a good option but I was pretty certain he would not tell me anything. His loyalty to Laney was one of the things I liked about him. And he'd never break her trust. Not to me.

* * *

I wasn't sure how late it was when our landline rang. I'd finally fallen asleep, drugged by the oppressive heat. I'd expected to hear Laney on the other end, but instead it was Niklas.

"Sorry to disturb, but I was hoping Laney could help me with a phone number."

Even now, he still never greeted me when I answered or called me by name. I don't suppose he ever would.

I ran my hand over my mouth. "Laney's not here." I didn't want to say anything. If he knew she'd left me, Niklas would probably smirk to himself and think nothing of telling me I deserved it. "I could tell her to—"

"I'll call her tomorrow." Niklas cut me off. "Or I'll call her mobile."

"She's not really checking her mobile..."

"Why? Is she alright?"

"She's fine. She's away for the weekend with the girls..." It was too easy to lie to him. I hated lying, but he was the last person I would ever tell that Laney was gone and that I didn't know when she was coming back.

"Honestly, Mads? You think I want to keep talking to you, making small talk with you?"

"I only offered to help. I'm not asking you to give me an update on your life."

I waited for him to say something, anything. I could hear him breathing, so I knew he was still on the line. How often did he call? Was this another one of the details of my wife's life that I'd missed? That her ex still called and felt comfortable enough to do so, even late at night. Where had I been when all of this was going on?

"Do you have Anton and Ingrid's phone number?" he finally said. "I've found a host for Sasha."

"A host?"

"Laney didn't tell you?"

This time I said nothing. I waited.

"This is rich. I thought you two told one another everything. Laney always makes it sound like you know everything about one another because of your special... connection."

This time I cut him off before he could rub more salt into my wounds. I rattled off Anton and Ingrid's number and hoped they wouldn't confide in Niklas. I didn't think they would.

The worst part was that I almost wished Laney had gone to him. At least I'd know for sure where she was. And Niklas, as much as he hated me for taking Laney away from him, still loved her. It didn't matter that he was married to someone else. He still loved Laney.

* * *

On Saturday I was too restless to sit at home all morning. I went out for a run and then ended up at the workshop. The lights were on already when I arrived and Led Zeppelin's "Whole Lotta Love" was echoing through the space. I called out for Jonas and Morten, but the music was too loud. But neither of my workshop mates was there working on a Saturday.

It was Benny. She was bent over Jonas's drafting table, scribbling notes on what looked like the designs she'd shown us for a credenza. Instead of wearing her hair loose as she usually did, she'd pulled it into a messy topknot. It reminded me too much of Laney, of how she'd stretch her slender brown arms and then twist her hair, sometimes into a ponytail or a bun...but at night, always a topknot with stray tendrils of curls escaping from it. I blinked quickly. I didn't want Benny to remind me of Laney...I didn't want Benny in my head at all. Yes, she was attractive, and she was the sort of eye candy we men say we always want, but when it came down to it, the only woman who had the power to bring me to my knees was my wife.

Benny looked up from her designs. The smile she flashed at me—surprised, then almost flirtatious—caught me off guard. Anton's warning—that Benny was interested in me—blinked in my head. "I thought I'd have the place to myself," she said by way of explanation. She set down her pen. She was wearing one of those wife beater-style tank tops and it was obvious she wasn't wearing a bra. Her nipples pressed against the fabric. When she moved, her breasts swayed. I looked away, told myself to stay focused. I didn't want to be reminded of Laney asking me if I was attracted to Benny. Then, I hadn't answered her. I hadn't wanted to admit that there times when her overt sexiness affected me. Admitting it wouldn't have solved anything. It wouldn't have made

Laney come back to me. It wouldn't have convinced her I still loved her or that she was the only woman I wanted.

I nodded at her and then ventured to the back of the workshop where I always worked. It was better if there was distance between us. I focused instead on going through the design revisions the hotel group had requested. I kept my phone within reach in case Laney called.

I wasn't sure how much time passed. Benny stayed on her side of the workshop; I stayed on mine. But it was impossible to ignore her completely. She'd walk past, humming. Or she'd call out questions about some technique that she wanted to try for designing a joinery system for a table with wishbone legs. She knew how to get your attention. Benny made just enough noise, like a low frequency constantly registering in your thoughts. *Focus*, I reminded myself, each time she distracted me. *She is not who you want or need.*

"Listen...it's getting late, and I was thinking about heading across the bridge for a beer." Benny perched on the edge of my desk.

"I need to finish this," I said. "Big meeting on Monday."

"Come on, Mads. I heard you were home alone, so it's not like you have to rush home."

"What? Who told you...?"

She grinned at me. "Jonas said your wife went to the States."

"She's visiting her aunt. She'll be back soon."

"So you could go out for a drink then. You look like you could use some company."

"No," I retorted. I pushed back my chair and stood up. "I should head home anyway. Laney's going to call me—"

"I'm not going to bite, Mads. It's just one beer, and we're both heading the same direction." Benny slid off my desk now. She shrugged at me and then started walking towards the front of the workshop.

One beer... if it were Anton or Willem and Ibrahim, I would have said yes immediately. We'd have locked up for the night and then headed across the bridge to Nørrebro or Fredriksberg to have a beer and blow off steam. But Anton's warning was still fresh in my mind. And Laney's reaction to seeing me with Benny was still a raw reminder of everything I stood to lose if someone like her ripped a hole in my life. Keeping things professional was the only option. I picked up the design prints and then put them away for safekeeping.

We closed up shop and then headed towards Dronning Louises Bro. The thick heat pressed into my skin.

"Are you coming with me?" Benny asked as she fell into step beside me. We were halfway across the bridge.

I shook my head. "I don't think so. I've got..."

"She's got you whipped, hasn't she?"

"Don't talk like that about my wife."

"Sorry—I only meant it as a joke."

"I don't think it's funny. And I'm your boss—not one of your friends or your drinking buddies."

Sortedam Dossering was just ahead. Benny muttered out an apology as the bus to Husum drove by. I made to turn but then she grabbed my arm.

"So are we having this beer or what?"

"No, Benny, we're not..."

She laughed and shook her head. "Okay, suit yourself." Then she caught me off guard and kissed me quickly on the mouth—I stumbled backwards and put my hands out to push her away, but she backed off again, laughing, and said, "You can't blame me for trying."

"What the hell are you doing?" I stammered.

"You can't blame me for trying," she said again and laughed.

"No...no...fucking hell, Benny—I'm married. I love my wife. And whatever you think is happening between us—it's not going to happen."

She raised her eyebrows at me and then shrugged. "Suit yourself." Then she walked away, heading up Nørrebrogade. I wiped the back of my hand across my lips.

Fucking hell...Anton was right.

CHAPTER SEVEN: Laney

Namaste

Getting Liv to take a nap after her phone call with Mads proved difficult. Just speaking to him had made her so hyper that even my aunt was overwhelmed by the amount of energy my four-year-old could muster. We finally took her to the beach just so she could run and let off some steam. While she ran ahead of us, my aunt and I walked with Freya. Aunt Cecilia was curious to know how the call went. "Did you speak to him?" she asked as soon as Liv found a playmate on the beach.

"Only briefly." I shook out the beach blanket and busied myself with arranging it. Somehow, hearing Mads's voice again felt too fresh. I didn't want to dissect the short conversation we'd had. I'd kept my voice neutral, but inside I was screaming, "I love you—why can't I get over you? Why do I love you so much?" But that was that was the thing—I didn't want to get over Mads. I knew I was weak for him. Ever since that first time we met. He'd glamoured me and he was all I saw.

Cecily and I settled on the blanket and watched as Freya played with her sand bucket and spade. Liv bounded over, now bored with her new playmate. She plopped down beside Freya and planted a wet kiss on her little sister's cheek. As my daughters played, I finally confessed to my aunt how it felt to speak to Mads again after nearly a week of only text messages. "I fall every time I hear his voice." I kept my voice low, not wanting Liv to figure out we were talking about her father. "I love him too much, I think that's the problem."

"Sometimes we love too hard." My aunt reached for my hand. "I think you both love too hard, but you've forgotten how to be together."

Liv turned and watched us. She bit her lip and scrunched up her eyebrows. "Mommy, can I talk to Papa tomorrow as well?"

"Maybe," I said. "I can check with Daddy."

Once Liv was satisfied with my answer, she continued playing with Freya and the sand bucket. She sang to her little sister and told her how she'd spoken to their father. My aunt squeezed my hand. "While you're here, I want you to focus on feeling better...but don't give up on your marriage, Laney. Mads isn't perfect, neither are you."

"I don't want him to be perfect. I just want him to show me he wants to be part of our family."

"He does it in his way..."

"He's hardly ever around."

"He is trying to make a living for you and the girls."

"Are you playing devil's advocate or trying to annoy me now?"

"Devil's advocate, my darling." My aunt reached into her tote bag and pulled out a pair of oversized sunglasses. "I don't want you to make any hasty decisions. I want you to think about what you want. Which is why it's good you're going to come to the yoga course with Freya."

Though I pretended I wasn't paying attention, I took in everything Cecily said. She was my mother now. She was the one person who loved me when the rest of my father's family turned their backs on my mother and me. And when my mother died, Cecily found me and gave me a home. If there was anyone in this world I trusted, it was her. I knew she wanted what was best for Freya, Liv and me. I also knew she liked Mads. That was the problem, wasn't it? Everyone liked him. Men, women...especially women. It was not easy to be married to someone whom everyone adored or wanted.

"There's a girl who works with Mads..." I started. I wasn't sure how to broach the subject with my aunt. A lump was already forming in my throat as I tried to get the words out. I fidgeted with my wedding ring, twisting it round my ring finger, revealing a slim band of paler skin. "I know she wants Mads. And I'm scared that maybe he wants her too."

"Is this what pushed you over the edge?"

I nodded, but didn't make eye contact with my aunt. Instead, I focused on the girls. Freya had found shells in the sand and was trying to put them in the bucket. Liv was scooping sand with the plastic spade and pouring it over the shells. Any moment now a tantrum could erupt. Freya's bottom lip was already beginning to wobble. And Liv got a stubborn look on her face—the same one her father sometimes flashed when he'd already decided to do something no matter what anyone else said. But Aunt Cecily distracted Freya by jangling a set of keys. When she had Freya's attention, she reached in her bag and handed her a rubber duck. Before Liv could grab it away, my aunt handed her her own rubber duck. Tantrum avoided.

"How did you know to do that?" I asked. "I never figure these things out. The tantrums explode; I get nervous, just make things worse..."

"It's just back-up toys. They don't always work." Cecily stretched out her legs now and brushed kernels of sand from her dark skin. "Now tell me. Who is this woman who's got her sights set on your husband?"

"Her name's Benedikte, but she calls herself Benny." Her name felt ugly and sour in my mouth. I grimaced. "She's a furniture design student from one of the local colleges and she looks like the only thing she was made for was sex."

"And you think Mads is attracted to her."

"He didn't even mention her from the beginning. She's been working with him for months and the only one of the interns he ever told me about was Willem—"

"Is that another woman?"

"No, Willem's a guy. He's from Holland. He's been working there for around six months." I watched as Freya abandoned the bucket and crawled across the blanket to me. She looked tired. She hadn't wanted to nap earlier either but now looked hot and exasperated. I reached for her and settled her on to my lap. My aunt rummaged through my tote bag until she found Freya's favorite sippy cup. I'd filled it with apple juice before we left the house. While Freya drank her apple juice, I rocked her, hoping the slow motions would lull her into a nap. Liv commandeered the bucket now and filled it with more sand and shells as she sang about foxes.

"She kissed him, he came home with her lipstick on his cheek and on his neck. He said she was just congratulating him on winning a contract but even before that—when he forgot about our date and I showed up at the workshop—I saw how he was looking at her...and how she was looking at him like he was this prize she was going to reel in. I don't know if anything else has happened." I lowered my voice. "For all I know, he could be fucking her right now."

"Laney, don't jump to conclusions. Do you know for sure that something has happened between them?"

"She kissed him. I saw the evidence of it. I asked him if he was attracted to her and he wouldn't answer me."

"He won't act on it."

"How can you be so sure when I'm not even sure?"

"He's scared he's losing you. Your leaving him? You gave him a wake-up call. He knows he needs to fight for his family."

"He doesn't know anything. He doesn't even know we're here. He just knows we're okay."

"Laney, you can't do this to him."

"It's done."

"You need to tell him where you are. You need to give him a chance to come here and make things right. At the very least, you need to let him know where his kids are."

"You're on his side, then..."

"My darling, I am always on your side. But I want you to think about how you'd feel if he simply disappeared with your children and refused to tell you where he was."

Freya knocked the back of her head against my chest. She tipped her head back and sang "Mama" at me. She was such a happy little girl. And sometimes it hurt to look at her. Especially now when her green eyes reminded me too much of her father. Oh God...my aunt was right. No matter how angry I was...I had no right to keep him from knowing where I was or how he could find his kids. And Aunt Cecily was right—Mads would never do this to me. He would never walk out without telling me where he was going. He would never snatch the children away and take off. He might not be perfect but he would never be so selfish. But a part of me still whispered, he pushed you to this. His thoughtlessness, his assuming he could carry on with life without having to take any real responsibility with raising our children...letting his dreams take precedence over our family...and turning a blind eye to how much I was struggling to cope. And yet...there were those evenings when, even if he was late, he would go in to the girls' room and read to them or the Saturday mornings when he'd let me sleep in and take them to Tivoli, even though he hated all the crowds. And when Liv had nightmares, he'd go bring her to our bed and she'd lie between us as he murmured reassurances to her that there were no monsters under her bed, no witches waiting to eat her. That nothing bad would ever happen to her because he would always love and protect her.

I pressed a kiss to her forehead and she patted my cheek with her sticky hand. I was sure I now had sand stuck to my skin, but it was moments like this when I understood how much love I had inside of me for my youngest daughter. I could hold her like this while she giggled happily and bounced on my legs. She sang to me and blew spit bubbles and called out random words she managed to say. Sometimes it was simply "mama" or "dada"...lately she'd taken to saying "peen-gee"—which Liv said was "penguin"—she was probably right. If there was anything in this world that Freya loved, it was penguins. And Mads...he indulged her love of penguins. He carved and painted wooden penguins for her. He took her to *Det Blå Planet*, the aquarium near the airport, so she could see the penguins swimming around in the tanks. I had to remind myself that he did these things; he didn't simply abandon me. He loved his children...he probably loved them more than he loved me, and I was okay with that. Wasn't that how it was supposed to be? But...I still needed his love, I still needed to know he loved me and wanted me and that we were a team...that we really were in it for the long run.

Later, when we'd walked back to my aunt's house and had dinner on her back porch, I bathed the girls and asked them if they were happy they'd had a chance to speak to their father. Liv nodded and splashed me with water. "Papa sounded sad," Liv said in Danish. "He said he misses me."

"He does." I said as I shook out her bath towel. My aunt had found towels with penguin and fox prints for the girls.

"He said he miss you too, Mommy." She held up her arms and I lifted her out of the tub. I tried to keep my cool as I dried her off and helped her into her pajamas. Freya was still splashing in the tub. "You miss Papa too?"

I nodded. "I do..." Then I patted her bottom. "Now, go and give Gramma a kiss and then Freya and I will come in and we'll have a story."

Next, I took care of drying off a slippery and very wriggly Freya. I managed to get her into her pajamas before she got very far. Who knew a seven-month-old could be so quick—especially when she couldn't walk yet but was doing this scoot-crawl combo. After I cleaned up the bathroom, I found the girls on the floor, playing with the stuffed animals Cecily had given them.

"Which story tonight?"

"The fox..."

"Honey, we don't have that book with us...it's at home."

"I want the fox, though..."

So I made up a story for them. I told them about a fox who wandered far away from the forest and found herself in a big city where she didn't know anyone. "Was she scared?" Liv wondered. Her coppery eyes were wide with curiosity. She snuggled into me and clutched my arm. "I would be scared."

"Me too," I told her. Liv snaked her arm over my belly. "Even mommies get scared sometimes."

"I protect you, Mommy."

I could just imagine Liv, dressed in her favorite fox pajamas and a cape, exhibiting her superhero powers as she sought to protect me from any danger. My fearless daughter. Just four years old and she thought she could save the world. I hugged her and finished telling the story about the fox. As the story progressed, with the fox meeting a hippopotamus, a warthog and a weasel as well as a possum and a rhino, my aunt joined us. She'd also changed into her version of pajamas—silk loungewear I would have thought was far too glamorous for story time on the floor. So the story continued—our fox, who just happened to be named Bobbi Fox like Liv's favorite fox. I tried to come up with as many fun adventures as possible for the animal pals. Finally Liv yawned—her sleepiness winning the war of wills—and then she said, "This better than my other fox story."

"I'll tell you more tomorrow night," I promised as I pulled back the covers on her bed.

Liv scrambled into the bed and gave it a good bounce. "Promise?"

"Scout's honor." I bent down and gave her a good night kiss. I'd set my phone on her bedside table before I started the story; now it was blinking, and Mads's ringtone for text messages cut through the drowsy mood in the room.

Liv turned over on her belly and lifted her head, "Papa is calling, Mommy!"

I swiped my screen and read Mads's message: "There is no one else but you, Laney. I want to see you. I want to see our daughters. Please tell them I love them."

I knew Liv would not sleep until she had an idea of what her father said, so I told her that her father loved her very much.

"I love Papa too." She sighed. "Tell him, Mommy."

"I will, sweetie, I'll send him a message now." I typed in her message and then showed her the screen. Though she couldn't read yet, Liv nodded and said, "Good! Now Papa won't be so sad."

I kissed her good night and then turned off the lamp.

My aunt was singing a lullaby to Freya and had managed to get her into her toddler bed. She adjusted the safety rail and then tucked Freya in. Our daily visits to the playground and the beach seemed to tire her out enough that she drifted off pretty quickly every night. As we both left the room, my aunt paused to turn on the night lamp.

"I'm going to sit in the garden and enjoy the breeze," my aunt said. "Will you join me?"

I followed her out to the back porch. A breeze blew in from the ocean, fanning away the mosquitoes and cooling our skin. I showed Cecily Mads's message.

"Are you ready to forgive him?"

"I don't know...I think the problem is that I can't forget."

I didn't answer his message. I felt too raw, too exposed somehow to say anything that would reflect what was going on inside me. I wanted to tell him how being here, having my aunt's help with the girls—even if it had only been a few days—eased my mind. I wanted to tell him how this was what I needed from him. I wanted to tell him how calm I felt, how much I loved our daughters. I wanted to tell him how much I loved him... but I didn't know if I trusted him anymore.

As the house slept around me, I lay in my bed, windows open, and listened to the sound of the sea. I'd turned off the volume on my phone and set it to vibrate. It was after midnight here. In Denmark it would soon be time for Mads to get up. Would he go to the workshop to fill his day? Was he alone? Would Benny take advantage of my absence to try to get more out of him? I had the feeling she would. She didn't care about our marriage or our history. She wanted Mads.

I shouldn't have let any thoughts of her enter my mind. Whenever I thought about that moment—the hungry look on her face as she drank in whatever Mads had been saying to her...how she'd thrown back her shoulders and thrust out her chest so he would shift his focus to her rather prominent breasts...and he'd looked. Any red-blooded straight man would. But...he'd looked and I was sure he'd smiled. Maybe he'd liked what he'd seen.

I turned off the lamp and waited for sleep to come. Instead, my phone vibrated. I pulled it from under my pillow and swiped the screen. Another message from Mads: "Do you still love me?"

I could almost hear him asking me this. I could imagine him sitting here in this room, his head bent, his forearms resting on his knees as he leaned forward. I wished I could hear his voice. If I called him...but no, instead I answered him with honesty and brevity: "Yes."

* * *

I couldn't continue moping. I'd been here for over a week and it wasn't doing me any good, so I got up early and ate breakfast and watched the sun rise. Then I went for a jog along the beach and marveled at the shells sparkling in the sand. By the time I arrived back at the house, my mind felt clear and calm and I was ready to deal with getting a grumpy Liv up for breakfast. Freya was easier in the morning. She was usually already awake when I went into their bedroom, ready for whatever breakfast had in store for her. She was not so interested in breastfeeding now that she had a few teeth coming through. She was much more interested in mashed bananas, oatmeal or scrambled eggs.

I managed to get both girls to eat their breakfasts, though Liv complained and said she hated everything on her plate. I ignored her protests and drank my coffee. She cried, she screamed and threw her mashed bananas on the floor. I sipped my coffee and tried to focus on what was important. It did not matter if she had a tantrum about breakfast. I'd clean up the bananas from the floor once I'd finished my sandwich. When she was hungry, she'd eat. And she did. It didn't take long for Liv to realize that I was not going to give her something different.

My aunt breezed in and told me she'd see me at the studio later. She said this every day but so far I'd not gone. Now I felt like I was ready. And, while Liv finally gave in to eating, I called Peyton on the number my aunt had scribbled on a pad of Post-it notes and asked her if she could come over today to babysit.

My aunt's yoga studio was on Dogwood Street, just off Main Street. It occupied a beautiful old Spanish Colonial Revival house that had once been a speakeasy, the summer house of a 1940s starlet (or so rumors went) and then a restaurant. Later it had been rezoned and repurposed to retail space. When my aunt found it a few months after moving to Juno Beach, it was in a sorry state. But she'd renovated it, restored its beauty and created a perfect space to relax and reconnect.

I'd walked there, pushing Freya in the travel stroller I'd brought with me. She'd chattered the whole way. Sometimes I'd picked out a few words—"dada" and "sun"..."kit-kay" when she pointed to a particularly fat tabby cat sloping along the hedges of a house we passed. By the time we arrived at Namaste, my aunt's studio, my legs were tired but the walk had done me good. I could feel the blood pulsing through my limbs and I felt alive. Maybe some of the sluggish fog was finally lifting.

Inside, I parked Freya's stroller in the designated area, folding it so it wouldn't take up so much space, and then let Freya, who was kicking her legs excitedly, down onto the floor and walked slowly to the check-in desk. Freya scooted after me, singing as she followed me.

The woman who greeted us had one of the friendliest smiles I'd seen since I'd arrived in Florida. She stepped from behind the desk and asked me if I was here to take a class or just receive information.

"I was going to take a class," I said and waited for Freya to catch up with me. "My aunt—Cecily—she's the owner, and she thought I needed to take one of the classes."

I rummaged in my tote bag and handed her my Danish ID card. I'd lived outside the US for so long that the only form of American identification I held that was still valid was my passport. She scanned my ID card. "What language is this?"

"It's Danish—"

"Are you Laney? Ah, you must be Cecily's niece—the one from Denmark! My daughter Peyton is babysitting for you, right? I'm Rebecca." She handed my ID card back to me. "Cecily said you might be coming by."

"Hi...and this is Freya, my youngest daughter." Rebecca bent down and greeted Freya with an "Aren't you a cutie?," which Freya met with wide-eyed wonder. She wasn't a shy baby, but she wasn't really used to anyone other than me or Eddy speaking English with her. Mads always spoke Danish with her.

"Are you going to do the Mommy and Baby yoga class?"

I nodded. "My aunt thought it would be good for us." I wasn't sure how much Rebecca knew. Cecily was not one who gossiped but she might have shared with her neighbor and co-worker some of what was going on. "I've had a hard time...adjusting."

"Don't worry, I think most of the people who come to this pass have been in the same situation. And honestly, the Mommy and Baby classes pretty much saved my life when I first moved here."

"Really?"

"It's a long story," she said and laughed. "I'll tell you about it later. Cecily invited me and the girls over for dinner, so I can fill you in then."

Rebecca showed me which room the Mommy and Baby yoga class would be in, then helped me with choosing a yoga mat for me and Freya. Once I was in the room, a smidgen of doubt crept in. What was I doing here? I'd done yoga in Stockholm and never really felt especially calm because of it. Often I'd spent too much time worrying that I could not hold the positions as well as some of the other women there. If Eddy were here, she'd laugh at how reticent I'd become. No, she would goad me until I at least gave it a try. And now, as I picked a spot near the front of the room, I channeled a little of my cousin's bravery. She'd been strangely silent since I'd told her I was leaving Mads. She was not in the easiest of positions—she was my cousin, and she was married to Mads's cousin. Her loyalties were divided. She wanted to support me; she liked Mads and wanted to support him as well. I'd tried not to go to her too often with my problems. It was embarrassing—dealing with the weight of this and not knowing what to think or do. I'd asked her once if she thought Mads would cheat on me but she'd laughed at me and said, "He's too in love with you and his girls to look at another woman." I didn't tell her about how he didn't show up for our anniversary date or how he'd come home with Benny's lipstick on his cheek and neck.

I sometimes wondered if this was payback. Payback for cheating on Niklas, for willingly fucking around on him and not caring about the consequences...but then Liv would giggle or I'd watch Freya playing with her Duplo blocks and suddenly I'd be reminded of how Mads had given me my girls. Without him, they would not be in my life.

While I was having my little existential crisis, other women had begun to enter the room and select spots. Some of them had infants strapped to their chests with in baby slings. Others had children around Freya's age with them. Two men joined the group. Both had infants with them. The cynic in me thought they were here to pick up women, even wondered if the babies were truly theirs. But then again...in Scandinavia, many men took parental leave and actively took a role in raising their children. It wasn't like it had been in my parents' marriage where my dad worked, came home and plopped in front of the TV and had no interest in children. Hell, for all I knew, they were a gay couple who were raising twins.

One of the men turned and nodded at me. I returned the nod and then glanced away, focusing instead on Freya, who was already trying to push herself into a yoga-like pose—pressing her hands into the mat and pushing herself upwards in her version of downward dog—though I was sure she was just trying to figure out how to stand up without help.

"She's a natural," the young woman who'd just taken the instructor's place at the front of the room. "A yoga natural!"

I looked down at my little girl, her rump in the air as she tried to balance. She toppled over on the mat and laughed. My heart swelled with joy.

As the class began, my nerves settled and I followed our instructor's directions as she guided us through each position. Throughout the class, she reminded us to make contact with our children—eye contact, a gentle touch...and with each position, I felt as though Freya and I were forging a closer bond. And the instructor encouraged us to look past the tears, the sleepless nights, remember that our children were the epitome of love. And Freya...she truly was conceived in love.

The night I think Freya was conceived, Mads and I were in Florence, Italy, for a romantic weekend away. We'd left Liv with Eddy and Henrik. It was one of our first weekend trips without her. I loved Florence—it was one of my favorite places in the world. The very first time I came to Europe, I started my trip in Florence and then took the train north until eventually I ended up in London to work. But Florence...every street hid some treasure—a leather shop that made the most beautiful journals...a *pasticceria* with perfect little confections that made you think you'd died and gone to heaven...churches so wondrous that even someone like me, who no longer believed in God, had a religious experience. I'd wanted to share this with Mads and when he suggested we have a weekend away, I took the lead and booked a three-day trip for us and splurged—taking some of my bonus money so we could stay in an upscale bed and breakfast near the Arno. We spent the first day overwhelmed by all the beauty around us—even with all the other annoying tourists who jostled us—but Mads held my hand and sometimes we'd find deserted streets and slowly stroll and then he'd stop and reel me in, taking my face in his hands and kissing me so deeply the only thing I could sense was our heartbeats in unison and longing streaming through me.

At some point I remember we lost our way. We could not remember which street would lead us back to our bed and breakfast. It was late and we'd had far too much *chianti classico* with our *bistecca fiorentina.* We ducked down alleys and side streets, looking for the entrance to the house but never finding it and that early spring night...when the air was so warm it felt like summer, though the Florentines were still bundled in down jackets... Mads gathered me in his arms in a deserted side street and kissed me so long and hard my knees buckled. I remember telling him how I wanted him to be the last man I ever made love to... and the smile that spread across his lips—so quick, so intense—made me fall even harder. His hands slid along my hips, gathering the folds of my skirt and spreading my legs with his thigh... I managed to stop him before we went too far... but I was so far gone, every fiber of me was attuned to this longing and wanted nothing more than for him to push me against a wall and lock my legs around him so he could take me... but I stopped him and laughed as I straightened my skirt and led him down one twisting street after another until we finally managed to find our little inn.

That night, we hung the "Do Not Disturb" sign on our door and we made love until our bodies were sore and too sensitive... and still we wanted more. I remember how we tried to be quiet whenever someone passed our room. I'd bite my lip and try to hold in the brazen longing, Mads buried his face in my neck as his fingers dug into my hips and held me still. The brass bed squeaked and groaned with each thrust... and all I knew was that my body screamed out to be touched and stroked and penetrated. His hair was longer then, and I remember how I raked my fingers through those red-gold strands and gripped him and we kept our eyes locked on one another... I came so hard, and a few minutes later so did he...and when afterwards I twined my arms around him and he was murmuring to me in Danish that being inside of me was like coming home, I had this sensation that something monumental had just happened... I wasn't sure what, but I remembered how my body felt so attuned to Mads's and how I almost felt like I could read his thoughts. My body was singing, *I love you, I love every inch of you, I love you*...and his body responded in kind.

Two months later, I found out I was pregnant.

* * *

Later, when we were home again, I paid Peyton and thanked her for taking such good care of Liv, who was at the kitchen table drawing a picture of what looked like sunflowers. Freya had fallen asleep on the way home. Apparently baby yoga had proved tiring for her, so I let her nap. I took her into my bedroom and laid her down on the bed. I sat down beside her and rubbed her back as she slept. My sleeping angel. Aunt Cecily was right...we needed that yoga class. And tomorrow...we'd go again.

CHAPTER EIGHT: Mads

Wisdom in a Glass

After work, Jonas and Morten convinced me to grab a beer or two with them and they pried it out of me—the situation with Laney and me. We'd started the evening at Kalaset, a café near the workshop. We'd said we'd only duck in and have a beer and a sandwich but once we started talking, one beer became two and two led to three.

"You think she's going to divorce you?" Jonas wondered as we each nursed our third beer. He scratched the top of his shaved head. "That would fucking suck, Mads. You've got this perfect life and you're about to lose it because of our collective?"

"I hope we're not anywhere near a divorce," I retorted, but what did I know? The few times I'd actually managed to talk to Laney, she made sure our conversations were brief and focused mostly on the girls. We'd been apart now for close to three weeks, and I didn't know what to think anymore. "But I need to figure it out. I don't want a divorce. I want us to work out the problems."

"Does Benny have anything to do with this?" Morten drained his glass.

"A little, yeah..."

"You're not fucking around with her, are you? Why would you even want to when you've already got such a sexy wife?" Morten demanded.

"I'm not fucking Benny," I clarified. "I think *she* wants it, but I am not going there. I love Laney. She's the only one I want."

"Good," Jonas said. "Otherwise I would have beaten the shit out of you. I like Laney a hell of a lot. Hell, I remember the first time she came by the workshop, I was all set to charm her and then I saw she only had eyes for you."

"So wait—if nothing's on with you and Benny, why does Laney think there is?"

"Benny kissed me on the night we signed the contracts for the hotel renovation. And then she kissed me again a couple of weeks ago. I turned her down. It's been pretty awkward, to say the least."

"This calls for another round," Jonas decided. He took care of ordering another round of pints.

"Dude, she knows you're married. She needs to step back." Morten looked more disturbed than anything else. "She was asking me all these questions about you a couple of weeks ago, but I thought it was just curiosity since we all work so closely. I didn't think she was going to start making a play for you."

"I don't think we can keep her on," I said. "It doesn't matter how good a designer or woodworker she is, she can't work with us and think it's okay to make a pass at me, or any of us for that matter."

Jonas returned with our beers. Morten drank his too quickly and then lurched outside for a cigarette. I remember following him and then the tight expression on his face and his hunched shoulders told me there was more going on. And then it came out—he was sleeping with Benny and had been for several weeks.

"She came to my place on Saturday night—so that must have been a couple hours after she asked you to go out for that beer..."

I lit a cigarette and listened as he let it out.

"She showed up at my place, she was already a little drunk and she was saying how some married guy was hot for her and she knew it and that it turned her on... fuck... all that time she was talking about you. I thought was talking about Anton, but I kept thinking he didn't even act like he liked having her around."

"I'm not hot for her. She's attractive—it's not like I haven't noticed that. And yeah, I looked, but it's difficult to ignore her but...I'm not interested in her."

"You think she's going to cause problems at the shop?"

"I don't know. I hope not, but Laney..."

"You tell her Benny kissed you a second time?"

I shook my head. "I think I should, though. I don't like keeping secrets from her."

"It might make things worse."

"How much worse can it get? My wife left me. She took my daughters with her. I miss them like crazy..."

"You might lose her for good." Morten took one last drag from his cigarette and then squashed it out. "But you know Laney better than I do."

At some point we left Kalaset and wandered across Fredensbro into Nørrebro. We'd tried to get a table outside at Nørrebro Brygghus but it was too crowded. We moved on then towards Fredriksberg and convinced Henrik and Eddy to meet us at Von Fressen, a German-inspired bar and restaurant not far from their apartment. Jonas and Morten were a good buffer, since Eddy was giving me the cold shoulder. I hadn't seen her in a couple of days and I could tell she'd talked to Laney in that time. At one point, she quipped at me, "Have you figured out where your wife is yet?"

I shook my head. "I'm going to call her tomorrow. We can't keep on like this."

"Have you tried asking her?"

"Of course I have! She won't tell me."

"Don't be so fucking clueless, Mads—where the hell do you think she is if she's in the US?"

"I don't know! OK? She could be anywhere—"

"She's with my mother! Okay? I can't believe you didn't figure that out...my mom's the only person she would go to there. How many times has she told you my mother is like *her* mother for Laney?"

Then she snatched my phone from me and tapped in her mother's number. "Use it tomorrow," she said. "And stop being so goddamn thick. My god! What is wrong with you Scandinavian men?"

I woke feeling as though someone had sucked all the moisture out of my brain. For a minute the whole room spun. I closed my eyes again and breathed in and out slowly. Fuck...I was too old for this. When I opened my eyes again the world had decided to cooperate and stop spinning so much. But my mouth tasted sour and sticky. I pushed myself into a sitting position and blinked against the blinding sunlight streaming into the room.

This wasn't my bed. I still had all my clothes on... Shit...where was I? I tried to retrace my steps...

Drinks with Morten and Jonas...meeting Henrik and Eddy...

Right...I was at their place. I didn't remember much else. I think we had plenty more to drink. I was drowning my sorrows, Henrik took pity on me and let me sleep in their guest room. I didn't remember coming here. I probably became maudlin at some point in the evening. I managed to get out of bed and take a shower. Henrik left a clean T-shirt and boxer shorts on the bed. Which was good. Yesterday's shirt reeked of sweat and cigarette smoke. I would be glad when this heat wave ended. Even if the heat reminded me of that first time I met Laney...it always did... the heat, the humidity...the tiny beads of perspiration slowly sliding down her back...and that night in the hotel. Everything that was good in my life...it all started that night. And Laney...she was the one who gave it to me. And that's when it all clicked for me. Going to Milan? I couldn't do it. And I couldn't wait for Laney to tell me when she was ready for me to come to her. The longer I waited, the more time we left it, the further apart we'd grow. I couldn't leave this to chance.

I arrived early, unable to deal with the silence at home, but now at the workshop something felt off-kilter. Jonas and Morten weren't there yet—maybe they were still the worse for wear. They usually arrived first with takeaway coffee and read the newspaper at their conference table before starting the day. Benny was usually there too, but I was glad not to see her. After everything Morten had told me, I knew we were going to have to have an uncomfortable conversation, and I was hoping Anton would help me with it. The only person in the workspace besides me was Willem, who didn't look up from the prototype he was working on. His shoulders were hunched as he planed the wood. Further in the workshop, Anton was bending strips of wood. He'd designed a basket weave back for a chair and was testing which types of wood would best suit it. I nodded hello at him as I headed to the office. I sat down at the desk Anton and I shared and then checked my email. None of it was very interesting until I came upon one from a place called Namaste with the subject line "Compliments of Cecily." Cecily...? Then it clicked for me—Laney's aunt. I opened the message and there was a picture attached of Laney and the girls sitting on a striped beach blanket. In the background a terracotta lighthouse stood out against the blue sky. Laney was sitting cross-legged with Liv and Freya on her lap. Freya was peering up at Laney while Liv pointed at whomever had taken the photo and was laughing. My girls... I touched the screen, wishing I could reach through it and trail my fingers along the fine slope of Laney's cheek.

"I thought you should know they're safe and sound, here in Juno Beach, Florida, with me. They miss you, Mads. And they are here for you—but you need to show them you deserve them." The rest of the message was just as direct—Cecily gave me her address and telephone number and then signed off with "I know you love my niece. I'm counting on you to do good by her."

I swallowed hard then looked down at my hands. My wedding band was askew, revealing a pale strip of skin. On Saturday it would be four years...and I was supposed to be in Milan. Christ, what was I thinking?

When I looked up, Anton was in the doorway, shaking sawdust out of his dark, curly hair.

"I'm not going to Milan," I said. "I think you should go instead."

"What are you going to do?"

"I know where Laney is now...so I'm going there."

"I was wondering when you'd finally come to your senses." Anton strode into the room and then sat on the edge of the desk. "Did she ask you to come?"

"No...I'm not waiting for that. I don't want to be without her. And it's our anniversary on Saturday...I can't fucking believe I was going to go to Milan instead of celebrating it with her. What the fuck is wrong with me?" I cradled my face in my hands. "I'm an idiot..."

Anton didn't contradict me. "You want me to go instead?"

"Yeah, as long as Ingrid's okay with it."

"You should book your ticket, then...if you're going to America."

"We can tell everyone after the meeting."

The meeting with Ole and his minions went as well as could be expected. We presented the revised sketches; they said they were perfect and then requested further changes. I maintained a poker face—it was the only way to get through these meetings, but Jonas and Morten were quick to let their frustration show. At one point, Jonas demanded to know what kind of game Ole was playing. "Why the hell did you accept our bid and our designs if you want to water them down until they're nothing but copies of something everyone else has already done?"

And Ole, pragmatic as always, answered, "We wanted the best...and now we want you to be even better."

When our clients were gone and it was just the team left in the workshop, I told them the news about Milan. "I can't go, not when I need to take care of things with my family. And they come first. They always come first."

"I can't believe you would throw away such an honor," Benny said. She was the only person at the table who disagreed with my decision.

"*Hold kæft*, Benedikte!" Willem muttered. "It's Mads's decision—not yours."

"It's a stupid decision—this whole collective is on its way to being the new wave of Danish furniture design and he's going to soothe some woman's ego?" The longer she spoke, the more I wished she'd stop. I could already feel my fingers tightening into fists. "I don't see why it can't wait another wee—"

"Enough, Benedikte!" I couldn't stand to listen to her any longer. I slammed my palm on the rough tabletop. "I don't give a shit if you don't agree with my decision! You don't like it? There are other places to work!"

No one said anything for a long time. I was still bristling with rage at Benny's presumption. I stared her down—surely she wouldn't continue to spout off. But she didn't seem to have any common sense. Instead, she continued, "What about the exposure the forum will bring to you?"

"*Fanden*, Benny!" Now Willem lost his patience. "Give it up—you already tried to fuck Mads, everyone knows it! He doesn't want you! You've already fucked nearly everyone here, and now you're acting like the only thing you care about is the collective?"

She let out an exasperated groan and folded her arms across her chest. "Asshole..."

"Benny, I think you should go home," I said finally. I'd had enough of this. "Just...go."

"Are you firing me?"

"Yeah, I am. We'll pay your notice period. But...just go."

She looked around wildly—I think she thought someone would stand up for her, but no one came to her defense. She pushed back her chair. It scraped the floor and when she stood up, her chair tipped backwards.

"Fuck you—fuck all of you!" She stormed away from the table and then gathered her sketchpads from her drafting table. None of us moved from the table. Not until she finally stalked out of the workshop did we leave the table. The tension coiling inside me finally unfurled. In a way, it felt as though the workshop had been holding its breath, and now it had dared to exhale.

"So when do you leave?" Anton was the first to speak. He fell into step beside me as we headed toward our office at the back of the shop. "Did you even get a chance to book your ticket?"

I shook my head. "I'm going to do it now. I don't want to wait. I feel like I lost enough time already."

"Ingrid and I were starting to wonder if you were giving up."

"I love Laney too much to give up."

"Good. Because if you'd given up...and if you'd fallen for Benny's tricks...I swear, I would have kicked your ass."

* * *

By the time we closed up for the day, I felt more like the old me. I wasn't obsessing over the designs or if Ole was going to come up with new demands for changes. I wasn't even worrying about if there would be any repercussions from firing Benny. I could almost hear Anton saying, "I knew she was going to be trouble..."
I could even remember the uncertain expression on Laney's face as she asked me if I was attracted to Benny. Why hadn't I answered her? Why hadn't I just said no?

I knew the answer.

I was afraid she wouldn't believe me no matter what I said. Benny was never who I wanted. She knew how to get under my skin–under everyone's skin. She'd intrigued me–she was so free, she did what she wanted, said what she wanted. She reminded me of the way I used to be. But...she wasn't Laney. She was never the person whose very being I craved. Everything would have been easier if I'd just said no when Laney asked me. I was just too blind to see it.

I was still thinking about it as I walked home. For the first time in weeks the sky was clotted with heavy grey clouds. Thunder rumbled in the distance and the air was so heavy it nearly hurt to breathe. I managed to make it to the entrance to my building before it finally started raining. I climbed the flights of stairs to the apartment and then opened every window to let some fresh air in. If Laney were here, she would have opened all the windows too. She would say the rain was washing away all the stale air and was making everything fresh again. But it could never wash away Laney and how she made me feel.

While the rain pelted the city, I turned on Laney's iMac and booked my airline ticket. The best one I could find on such short notice was with Norwegian. I thought I'd have to fly via Oslo, but it was a direct flight to Miami International Airport. I also arranged for a rental car. I knew Florida would not be as easy to get around in without a car as New York. It was one of the things Cecily had told me about the last time she'd visited us.

Once everything was booked, I called Laney. It was around lunchtime on the East Coast of America. I tried to imagine what she was doing as I waited for her to pick up. Was she at the beach with our daughters? Were she and Cecily having one of their heart-to-heart conversations? Was it raining in Florida as well? Mostly though, I wondered how she would react when I was finally there. I hoped she would not be indifferent. I hoped she would not look at me with the same disappointment shining in her eyes. I wanted her to see me and still feel that same pull, the longing, the intimacy, I wanted her to remember that we were good together, and that we could still be good together. Most of all, I wanted her to remember that she loved me.

I didn't want to leave another voicemail. Instead, I sent a text message that summed up everything going through me.

"*I'm sorry I didn't pay more attention to what you were going through. I promised you I'd always be there. And I broke my promise. I'm sorry.*"

All I Want

The sun was just rising, casting a silvery glow to the colorless sky. The higher it rose, the clouds in the distance warmed to rosy tints of gold. I stopped, let my toes sink into the wet sand and watched the sky come to life. Rebecca was right—coming to the beach every morning and walking along the shoreline, listening to the waves and letting them splash my feet was the best form of medicine for me.

Over dinner last night, she'd shared her story with me—how she left behind an abusive husband and a marriage gone wrong to save herself and her daughters. "I didn't even know where I was going," she'd said as the citronella candles flickered on the painted porch railing. "I asked Peyton and Lorelei what they wanted most, and they said they wanted to see the ocean. So we ended up here."

"Did you know anyone here?" The night had gone chilly and we'd both borrowed shawls from my aunt.

Still, we shivered a little, but it was so relaxing to sit here talking like old friends, even though we'd only just met.

Rebecca shook her head. "Nope, no one. Aside from the staff at the motel where we were staying while we tried to find a place to live, your aunt was the first person I met. I was going around trying to find a job, and she said I looked like the sort of person who could use a good break."

"That sounds like Cecily through and through," I said. A moth fluttered over my head and I fanned it away. "She rescued me from foster care when my dad refused to assume custody of me. My mom had died, and I didn't have anyone. And my aunt found me."

"When was that?"

"I was fifteen when my mother found out her breast cancer was terminal...and then three months later she died." I knew my voice sounded strangely detached as I told Rebecca my story. Sometimes it felt like it had happened to someone else. But the memory of it still lived within me. I never realized how much I needed my mother until she was gone, when suddenly I was a ward of the state and my father would not take me in. "I don't want my girls to ever go through that...the uncertainty, not knowing they are loved..."

"I think they know," Rebecca assured me. "Peyton said Liv kept talking about her papa...she couldn't understand everything, but...she said Liv sang a song about how she loved her daddy."

I nodded and laughed. "Yes, that sounds like Liv. She adores her father."

"But he's not here...?"

"No...I'm...taking a break."

"Cecily mentioned it." Rebecca hugged her knees. "She said you needed some time to think things through."

"That's about the size of it."

"Are you thinking about getting a divorce?"

"I don't know...I don't know anything. I don't want my marriage to be over...but I don't want it to be the way that it is now."

"You should meditate... when you walk on the beach, just repeat some affirmations to yourself, to remind you of what's important...of what you want."

"It's that easy?"

She nodded. "I do it whenever I feel confused, or stuck. I run, I run in the evening and I let my mind wander and then I think through what I want or I remind myself of what's working in my life. You should try it."

So now I was doing it. Walking along the beach, letting my mind swirl with all the worries I kept inside. The air smelled like home—that familiar scent of wet sand, salt and the sea. It reminded me of those walks we took together. It didn't matter what time of year—Mads would wake up, anxious to make love...this I missed so much, how gentle it could all start and then the ache, the desire took over...afterwards we'd linger in bed, have a lazy breakfast and then we'd take the train or drive to the sea. Sometimes we were the only ones on the beach...and he'd walk ahead, always looking back and stretching his hand out to me and calling my name, calling out, "Laney...come...I want to show you something..." His strong hands clasping mine... and in winter, when his beard grew in thick and coppery, how I'd rub my cheeks against his and those red-gold hairs would tickle my skin.

I want...I want to feel whole again...I want the waves to wash away my doubts. I want to be loved. I want him to love me, I want to love him again... I want to love my children... I *do* love my children.

Saying this...whispering it to myself as I walked in the sand...how silly I felt at first. But the longer I walked, the more these words felt like they were true. They *were* true. And in my mind they transformed. *I am whole. I love myself. I love my children...I love my husband. I am whole. I am healed.*

It is true. It *will* be true.

I returned to my aunt's house feeling unburdened. My aunt and my daughters were still sleeping, and the house seemed as caught in slumber as they were. I checked on the girls. Liv's small body barely made a hump in her bed, though her uncontrollable curls formed a halo on her pillow. Little Freya sighed and murmured as she turned over. I crossed the hall to my room and closed the door behind me. Rebecca was right. I did feel better. And

I'd made a decision—at least about whether I would return to work early. I didn't want to lose these months with Freya and Liv. Even if it meant that I would lose my job—I would think of something. I could even freelance—I'd done it before, I could do it again.

I retrieved my iPad and began typing in my letter of resignation and pressed send before I could change my mind.

* * *

"Ah, good! You're still here!"

I'd just finished wiping down my yoga mat and was rolling it up when my aunt found me. Freya had waddled over to the window and was watching a group of kids play in Namaste's back garden.

"Yeah, we're still here," I said and slipped my yoga mat into its pouch. "I was going to take Freya to the park, but we can stick around if you need help."

"I do," Cecily gestured at the group of children outside. "Do you think you could help me with a kids' yoga session?"

I wasn't sure how much help I could be. I wasn't very good at yoga. Practicing it made me feel better but I lacked the flexibility of Heaven, who led the Baby & Me yoga classes, and I didn't have my aunt's passion for it. I didn't want to say no, though. Especially since she'd been doing everything she could to help me and the girls. Instead of going out in the evenings for walks with her friends or having dinner with Otis, the man I knew she was dating though she pretended otherwise, Cecily was staying close to home, counseling me, consoling me.

"I could try." I housed the strap of my yoga bag on my shoulder and then scooped up Freya. "What shall we do with this little bundle in the meantime?"

"She'll be in the playgroup that Rebecca's taking care of." Cecily looked relieved. "Normally Heaven helps me, but she had a dentist's appointment scheduled."

"It's fine." I followed my aunt as she led the way to the garden. We stopped briefly to drop off Freya with the playgroup. I'd expected Freya to cling—she sometimes didn't take well to strangers, but she was used to Rebecca and, as soon as she saw the other children, she lost interest in me and squirmed to be let down to join them.

"Are we doing an outdoor session?"

"It's better for the group we're working with. Being out in the sun, hearing the birds and feeling the wind on their skin—it seems to calm them more than any soothing music ever could." Before she opened the door to the garden, she paused and added, "Some of these kids have been abandoned or abused, some of them just need a little attention. And they get what they need when they come here."

Outside, a group of preteen and teenage boys and girls waited. There were around ten of them and the older ones tried to look as though this was the last place they wanted to be. I knew that look so well. That had been me when Cecily first brought me to New York. I remembered being scared out of my mind—the city overwhelmed me, it was so much larger than Philadelphia, so many people, too much noise—but I plastered a bland, almost bored expression on my face and pretended that none of it touched me in any way. Cecily didn't buy it from me, and she certainly didn't buy it from them either.

She greeted them all by name. Some of them answered with, "Hey, Miss Cecily..." A few mumbled something similar. One or two remained icily silent.

"Is that all the enthusiasm I get today?" Cecily laughed and shook her head. "Now come on, get your mats and let's start."

Two of the girls giggled as they selected mats and chose spots, but the other three hung back. While Cecily unrolled her mat, I approached the trio and asked them if they needed any help.

"Who are you?" The boldest of the three jutted out her chin at me. She was shorter than me and stocky, while her friends were wisps of girls who tried to look tough.

"I'm Cecily's niece." I pointed to the basket of mats. "Do you need help setting up?"

The girl ignored me and called out to my aunt, "Miss Cecily, is this really your niece? She don't look like you."

My aunt planted her hands on her hips and laughed. "Sharee, are you going to give my niece a hard time, or are you going to get a mat?"

"We never seen her before though, Miss Cecily," Sharee retorted. "Where's Miss Heaven?"

"At the dentist's. Now come on, we haven't got all day—and my niece Laney is like a daughter to me, so be nice."

Sharee shrugged her shoulders and finally did as the others, going over to the basket and retrieving a mat. Her friends followed suit. I also rolled out a mat. I wasn't really sure yet what Cecily needed me to do, but I figured standing around wasn't really the point of it.

Once everyone was seated on their mats, Cecily instructed them to sit cross-legged and place their hands on their knees. Some of the boys awkwardly folded their long legs into the position and glanced around. My aunt had created a safe place for them. The garden was shaded from the street by tall, flowering shrubs and bamboo plants. She'd erected shade sails to keep the worst of the sun off the garden and provide privacy. As my aunt led them through the first breathing exercises, she reminded them to relax, to clear their minds and only focus on the joy inside them. After a while she lifted a small bell and rang it. She nodded at each teenager and asked them to repeat after her: "May I be safe...may I be happy... may I be well."

Around me, their voices formed one as they repeated the phrases my aunt intoned. She took them through a cycle of three repetitions then led them through sun salutations. I stood and observed, sometimes helping them adjust how they held their arms or legs, careful to ask if they needed help first. Some of them flinched when I spoke to them, no matter how soft a tone I used. One of the boys edged away from me when I tried to help him adjust his arms during the second round of sun salutations.

"I can do it," he muttered. He wouldn't look my way. "I don't like to be touched..."

"Okay, no problem," I assured him and then talked him through the position. His shoulders relaxed, but his breathing still sounded tense. I reminded him to focus on breathing slowly and letting his troubles disappear with each breath. After a while he nodded at me and whispered, "Thank you..."

Through each pose, my aunt spoke calmly to them, describing how to place their hands and feet, reminding them to find their center and stay focused on the here and now. I knew that once the session was over, she'd have a chat circle with them. As we went through the last cycle of yoga stances and chants, I stood back and watched how my aunt connected with her charges. She spoke to them in a soft, reassuring voice as she instructed them now to lie down on their backs, close their eyes and go to a safe place. I joined them, though I continued standing.

I let my mind wander to my safe place. When I was younger and my parents were arguing, I always dreamed myself away to a path in the forest. I liked the idea of wandering into this strange, green space. The trees towering over me, protecting me. I'd crawl under my bed with my pillow and hum to myself, until all I saw was the winding path, strewn with twigs and pebbles, the silvery white birch and the shadowy pine trees. I should have been frightened, but it was the forest of my dreams and I knew I was always safe.

I'd forgotten about my safe place. Shelved it away when I moved in with my aunt, bottled it up inside me and let it lie dormant. Now it spiraled again within me, reminding me that it could help me again...if I needed it. And I wouldn't need to run away to find it.

"Thanks so much for helping me today." Cecily and I were walking home now. I was pushing a napping Freya in the stroller, still a little stunned at remembering my childhood sanctuary. "Sometimes the kids can be a handful when I'm on my own, which is why Heaven usually helps me."

"They seemed pretty mellow today."

"We've had good sessions the last week or so," my aunt said as we stopped at the corner and waited for the traffic light to turn green. "It's taken a while to get to this point. All of them have had such fractured lives. A little like you have."

"Fractured...yeah, that would pretty much sum up most of my life." When I was with Niklas, I'd always kept that aspect of my life hidden. It unnerved him—despite his background as a therapist. He liked it when things were orderly, smooth and calm. With Mads, it was different. When I first told him about my broken background, he'd been more angry for me than scared of what it meant. He'd muttered a few choice Danish profanities as

I told him about being taken into foster care when my dad said he didn't want me in his life. He was the first person aside from Eddy and Aunt Cecily who'd reacted with such anger and frustration at my situation. And it cemented it for me—he was the one who would keep my heart safe.

As we started walking again, I could sense my aunt was trying to approach this from another angle. She kept making her usual "hmmm" sound as she tapped her left hand on her thigh. She always did that when she was thinking.

"Maybe you need to come to these sessions too," Cecily mused as we crossed the street. "You've been holding so much inside of you for too long."

"I don't want to sit in a circle with a bunch of kids," I countered.

"Laney, you need to meditate."

"No, not with them..."

"I should have made you do it when you first moved in with me all those years ago. You've needed it for so long."

"I don't want to talk about my marriage problems with those kids."

"You don't have to talk about your problems with them. Just meditate with them. You can talk about your problems with me."

"I already tell you..."

"I don't think you tell me everything that is bothering you," Cecily said. "Which makes me wonder how much you told Mads."

"I told him everything." I retorted.

"No, I don't think you did." By now we were only a few minutes from her house. My aunt's words rang through my mind. She knew me too well. She knew I wasn't always good at expressing my fears or my needs. If anyone understood this, Cecily did. "But sooner or later you're going to have to open up more, stop hiding things inside you. It doesn't help."

* * *

"How could you quit without telling us?" Johan's and Marius's faces filled my iPad screen. "You can't just leave us!"

"Hello to you too." I balanced my iPad on my knees. I was in the garden with Liv and Freya. Lorelei, Rebecca's youngest daughter, had come over earlier, wondering if the girls wanted to play. She and Liv were trying to catch butterflies while Freya played with her DuPlo blocks. All of the girls were in their bathing suits. I'd promised them they could run through the sprinklers once they were tired of chasing butterflies.

"Does this mean you aren't coming back to Denmark? Please tell me you haven't abandoned us to these crazy Danes!" Johan's voice went up an octave. It always did when he was nervous. It was one of the things Marius and I used to tease him about. Hearing it now made me miss working with my team.

"What makes you think I'm not in Denmark...?" Which was a stupid question to even ask. Mads had probably called them the moment he realized I was gone, trying to figure out what they might know—when the only thing I'd ever told them was that being at home with two small children was no walk in the park.

"Mads told us!" Johan barked at the screen. "He said you left him, said you took the kids—what the hell is going on? I thought you two were my friends who'd never get a divorce—"

"We're not getting a divorce..." Just thinking about a divorce made my chest tighten. I didn't think I wanted to go that far... Mads and I had issues...but I had to believe that we could find our way back to one another.

"You don't sound so certain," Marius quipped. He raked his fingers through his dark hair and gave me a stern look. "Tell me this is just a bump in the road."

"I don't know what it is...I think it's temporary. I just need to get my life on track—and Jens calling and saying I had to prove I was committed to my job—that my job was more important than my children...I just couldn't take it. I can't do that."

"I don't blame you, Laney," Marius admitted. "And...look, if you're not here, we're not here. We've been thinking about this for awhile."

"What are you talking about?"

"We're starting our own agency—and we want you to join us."

"But you're coming back?" Marius asked. I heard the caution in his voice.

"I haven't been gone that long." I reminded him. I'd only been here a couple of weeks, though it felt longer.

My maternity leave was another matter. I'd started it three weeks before Freya was born. If I still lived here in the US, I would have already been back in the office again.

Johan looked as though he was about to panic. "But you left Mads—"

"It's temporary, Johan. I needed a break. That's all." Lorelei and Liv threw down their butterfly nets and joined Freya on the lawn. I asked the girls if I should turn on the sprinklers now but they were much more interested in the inflatable wading pool my aunt had found. She was outside too now—in one of her fabulous fifties-style bathing suits and flip-flops. She'd already inflated the pool and was now filling it with water.

"Sounds like you're having a good time with the girls."

"I am. This time I've had with them so far...it's been really wonderful." I smiled as I watched Lorelei and Liv help Freya into the pool. My aunt gave Freya a rubber duck, while Liv and Lorelei sent streams of magic bubbles into the air with the bubble wands my aunt had found. Their laughter made everything feel right.

"But you're coming back?" Marius asked again.

I nodded slowly. This was just temporary. I had to remind myself of this. This was a vacation from my normal life. "Yes, I'm coming back...just not yet."

HAPTER TEN: Mads

Counting the Days

I was counting the days until I could leave for America. I'd never flown there before on my own—hell, I'd only ever been there twice and both times I'd gone with Laney. I didn't know I had to apply for a special entry visa—Eddy explained it to me after I'd received an email from the airline with the subject line: "Getting Ready for Your US Holiday". I called her as soon as I'd scanned it and come to the part about an entrance visa. Now she'd come to the workshop to help me fill it in.

"It's not really a visa," she said as she filled in the form. "And you should be filling this in yourself."

"You took over the computer," I reminded her, "and then you told me to go and pick up lunch for you. Which I've done." I slid her takeaway box towards her. "Roast beef *smørrebrød*, just like you asked for. And an iced tea."

"Did you go to that café Laney and I like?" She tapped the keyboard again.

I nodded. It was the same café I always went to and Laney swore by their iced tea. "I asked them to add extra mint, just like you asked."

"Done! Now you have your visa."

"*Tusen takk*, Eddy. I really appreciate this. I went into a panic as soon as I saw that mail."

"Didn't you have to fill out the last time you went?"

"I think Laney took care of it," I said. "I guess she took care of a lot of things I didn't think about."

Eddy and I were sitting at the farm table-*cum*-conference table. We had the workshop to ourselves. Willem and Ibrahim were on their way to Milan with Morten and Anton. Jonas had gone out to pick up his lunch. He was flying out to Milan tomorrow. Having her here made me feel like I had a better chance of convincing Laney to come home. I told myself Eddy wasn't pissed at me anymore, but I knew if I didn't get it right I wouldn't have her in my corner.

"I spoke to her last night," Eddy said as she cut her sandwich in half. She sectioned off a tiny square and then tasted it. "Ooh! This is yummy! I swear, this is better than those roast beef sandwiches I used to eat in Stockholm."

"Swedes don't know anything about *smørrebrød*." Which was definitely true. In the time I lived in Sweden, I never had a good open-faced sandwich. I gave up on them. "Or *wienerbrød,* for that matter."

"Have you told Laney you're going there?" I could see the concern etched on Eddy's face. She raised her index finger to her lips and tapped them with her fingertip. "Or were you planning on surprising her?"

"I haven't told her yet. Why? Do you think I should?"

"Well, sweetie, you should at least warn my mother that you're coming." Eddy shook her finger at me. "Cecily always like to be prepared."

"I'll call her tonight," I said. "Your mother, I mean. I think...I want to surprise Laney. Saturday is our actual anniversary. I thought...I'd show up, maybe she and I could have some time alone and just talk. Try to figure out where we are."

Eddy smiled finally, the stern look melting away. She reached across the table and took my hand in hers. "I know you want to make things right. And I want that, too. You and my cousin have been so good together. And I would hate to see that end."

"I don't want it to end," I assured her. "Everything that's good in my life is because of Laney."

"I think she'd say the same, sweetie." Eddy took another sip of her iced tea. She let out a sigh. "She wouldn't have Liv or Freya without you."

I missed my girls. I missed Freya's excited squeals whenever I lifted her in the air. I missed how Liv became my shadow as soon as I was home, following me everywhere, never letting me out of her sight as she filled me in on everything I'd missed during the day. It didn't matter where I was or what I was doing, she wanted to be there. "I hate going home to an empty apartment, it's not a home without them there. No Freya giggling or trying to find her balance...no Liv asking a zillion questions and climbing in my lap and telling me secrets..."

"They miss you, Mads. I'm glad you're going. You're doing the right thing—even if it means you won't be able to represent your work."

"I don't care about that. It started off as this dream I had, but I went into overdrive with it so I could support my family." I scratched my neck. It was a nervous tic. "I know what kind of life Laney had before she met me...I don't want her to ever feel like she's missed out on something because I can't support us."

"Does Laney know this?"

I nodded. "I let it get in the way, though."

"Well, try not to let it happen again." Then Eddy winked at me and grinned.

Once Eddy left, I focused on wrapping up as much as I could of my part of the hotel project. I'd just finished the changes Ole had requested to my design. I scanned everything into my computer and then sent the changes to Jonas, Morten and Anton to make sure they could continue with their own revisions. I checked my phone. No new messages, but it was still early in America. Jonas had just returned from lunch. He slammed into the workshop and let out a long stream of choice Danish swearwords.

I looked up from my drafting board. "What's happened?"

"Benny called me when I was having lunch."

"What did she want?"

"She wants her final paycheck...she wants it now, she wants us to write a good reference for her, she thinks you owe her an apology...she says we all do."

As Jonas continued with his list of Benny's wants, I felt my insides twist and knot. Anton was right. We should have never hired her, but we had to deal with it now. She was threatening to report us to the union. She said we'd discriminated against her because she was a woman.

"We could ask Anoushka to help," I finally said after Jonas finished listing all of our wrongs. I hadn't spoken to Anoushka in a few weeks. Sometimes she and Laney planned play dates for Lida and Liv. It was one of the strange webs of my life—that a little girl whom I helped create but was never supposed to have met would now be one of Liv's playmates. "If you think we're going to need legal help, she could give us some guidance."

"I shouldn't even be burdening you with this." Jonas knocked his fist on the stone wall. "You've already got enough to think about."

"Yeah, but this collective we've got—that's a big part of my life too."

"Look, just leave Anoushka's number and then Anton, Morten and I will take care of this. The last thing we need is Benny causing more problems for you and Laney."

I ran my palm over my mouth and leaned back in my chair. Had I sent out signals that I was interested in

Benny? I didn't remember anything specific. She'd flirted with every one of us when she first arrived in the workshop. Jonas had been the first one interested in her. He'd broken up with his long-term girlfriend, Zana, after months of what seemed like a cold war. And Benny had been there, every day, joking with Jonas, working on several projects... In the beginning she'd shown no interest in me. And that was fine. I was so busy then, with getting used to having a second child at home, at the cycle of sleepless nights that sometimes followed. I'd come to the workshop and fall asleep on the couch in the office during my coffee breaks. I think it was around the time when Laney and I thought Freya had colic. She'd wake screaming and we couldn't figure out how to comfort her. I think it was then that Laney and I began to drift apart, both of us exhausted from not having enough sleep, and then I threw myself into work.

"How long were you and Benny seeing each other?" I asked Jonas. It was something he'd never officially acknowledged, but we'd all known it was going on. The long lunch breaks they took, the evenings when they'd work overtime claiming they were behind schedule.

Jonas's neck flushed red. "Just a couple of months," he said and then changed the subject. But it didn't matter. All that mattered was that I'd be in Florida by Friday. And I'd be able to get my marriage back on track again.

* * *

I wasn't sure what to pack. I knew it was hot in Florida—wasn't it always summer there? My American trips so far had consisted of going to New York with Laney.

The first time we went, Liv was still a baby. We'd gone there to spend Thanksgiving with Eddy. It was easy to pack for that trip—winter coat, boots, thermal underwear, sweaters, jeans...it was freezing in New York, and the damp cold went straight through every layer of clothing you wore. One of the days we were there, we left Liv with Eddy and Henrik for the day and we took the train to Philadelphia. Laney wanted to put flowers on her mother's grave. She bought flowers—a bouquet of bright pink tulips—as soon as we'd arrived at 30th Street Station, then we took a taxi to the cemetery. It was just as cold in Philly as it had been in New York, and the taxi driver told us they were expecting snow. Laney said she'd pay him extra if he waited and turned off the meter. I remember thinking he'd agree and then leave us there, but he waited. And while Laney was arranging the flowers and telling me she knew they wouldn't last but they were her mother's favorites, it began to snow.

The second time we went Florida, but I didn't remember much of that trip other than getting sick already on the plane and being bed-ridden most of the week. Laney thought I had a stomach virus. I thought it was more likely bubonic plague. That trip was also in winter, but Laney had packed all of our bags. And since I spent most of the vacation either in the bathroom or in bed, I never really paid much attention to what I wore.

But Aunt Cecily and Laney took care of me, and Liv, who was only two then, crept into the bedroom at least twice a day to pat my arm and tell me she wanted me to feel better.

My empty suitcase lay open on the bedroom floor, waiting to be filled. So far, all I'd pulled out was a pair of linen pants and two black T-shirts. Well, it was a start, but it definitely wouldn't get me through two weeks in Florida. I'd booked a ticket with a flexible return date. I needed to be prepared for anything. Laney might turn me away. She might welcome me with open arms. I tried to read her whenever she arranged FaceTime calls for Liv and me, but she never let our conversations last very long. Sometimes Laney would sit in front the screen long enough to answer the questions I asked her—how was she, did she need anything from me, was everything okay with the girls...but she avoided looking at me, and when she did her eyes were glassy and she'd blink quickly and then rush to end the call. It didn't matter if I tried to convince her to stay a little longer, she'd find an excuse to end the call.

Last night she at least stayed on long enough to say "I love you..." Her voice was barely a whisper as she said it and it crept inside me and stayed with me all night. I dreamt she was lying beside me, her hand on my chest. I thought she was there, I thought I felt her lips on my skin, but when I woke up the room was empty. It almost made me feel worse...but I had to remind myself that I would see her soon.

When I finally finished packing, it was a little after midnight. It was still raining out and thunder was rumbling overhead. Lightning flashed outside the balcony doors. I stood by the doors and watched the rain slash down. It wasn't much longer until I'd be on my way. I just hoped she still wanted me in her life.

CHAPTER ELEVEN: Laney

True Confessions

"Mommy does yoga every morning," Liv announced as soon as Mads asked her how she was. "She goes for long walks too."

It was her daily FaceTime call with Mads. I told myself I was doing this for her—making sure she could spend time with him even if she could not actually be in the same place as him—but it was also for me. I wanted to hear his voice, wanted to hear him laugh at Liv's silly stories. I loved how he paid close attention to everything she said, he remembered what she told him and remembered to ask her questions about it.

"But that sounds nice," he said. "I'll bet Mommy is happy then."

I dared to glance up from the basket of laundry I was folding. Mads's tanned face...his hair was so much shorter now, it accentuated the sharpness of his cheekbones and nose. My breath caught in my throat... would I ever stop reacting to how beautiful he was? I didn't think he could see me, but then he raised his hand and waved at me. "*Hej, elskede...*"

I had no choice but to wave back and say "*hej.*"

"Your walks must be doing you good," he said as I came over to stand by Liv. I knelt beside her. On the other side of the ocean, Mads's smile broadened. "You look...happy."

"You cut your hair..." I blurted out without thinking.

Liv giggled and said, "Papa looks nice!"

"I didn't want it this short..." Mads grinned. He ran his hand over his newly shorn hair. His wedding band glinted in the light. "I said I wanted it trimmed...and the hair stylist went a little scissor-happy."

"It suits you." I wanted to reach through the screen and touch him. "It reminds me of those pictures from when you were younger...the ones your grandmother has on the wall..."

"Laney...when do you think you'll come home?"

His voice caressed me, grazing every sensitive bit of me and peeling away my defenses. I felt my will slip away. I could so easily fall. I knew I could.

"I can't...not yet." I braced my hand on the desktop. Liv leaned forward and kissed the screen. Mads leaned in too and pretended to kiss his screen. He closed his eyes long enough for me to drink him in. When he opened his eyes again, I couldn't look away. Neither could he. How long did we sit there, on opposite sides of the screen and the ocean, staring at one another, wanting one another too much? Thank God Liv was there to distract us.

"I love you, Papa..."

"I love you too, Liv." Mads blinked quickly and flashed a smile just for Liv.

"Papa, I can't find Bobbi Fox..." Liv pouted at the screen. She'd been surprisingly patient about Bobbi Fox's absence—especially since I told her enough Adventures of Bobbi Fox stories to convince her that Bobbi Fox was also on vacation and traveling the world. "I miss her."

Mads told her to hold on. He disappeared from the screen for a few moments and then he returned with Liv's stuffed fox and held her up for Liv to see. "Bobbi Fox came home, she thought Papa needed some company."

"Will you bring her with you?"

"Bring her?" He ran his fingertips over his lips. I thought I saw him smile, but maybe I just wished for it. I loved his smiles—loved how all the hard angles of his face softened and his eyes seemed to flare.

Liv nodded enthusiastically. "Mommy said you are coming too. She said you are coming soon."

Mads took this in. I saw how he glanced from Liv to me. Even if we were miles apart, he understood: we could not disappoint our daughter. "Bobbi told me she can't wait to see you again."

"When are you coming, Papa?"

"Soon, *lille ven*, sooner than you think."

"Say goodbye to Daddy now," I said to Liv. "I want to talk to him too."

At first Liv protested, but Mads calmed her down with a laugh and repeated his promise that he and Bobbi Fox would be there soon. She clapped her hands and blew him kisses. I helped her out of the chair and waited until I heard her chatting with my aunt.

"I miss you, Laney..." Mads said before I could begin wrapping up our call. He tapped the screen and left his hand there. "I want us to work through this. I told you...I'm in this with you for the long haul."

He'd said it to me so many times. Whenever we'd argued, whenever my doubts and insecurities flared and sent me running, he found me and he always said the same thing.

"Do you mean it?" I straightened my shoulders and tried to focus on him without letting my resolve falter. "Because if you're serious...about us, about staying together...then you need to come to me."

I tried to read the expression on his face—his eyes were cast down, a long shadow fell across the bridge of his nose. When he looked up again, he asked me if that was what I wanted, for him to come.

"I came to you, I put everything on the line for you," I said. "Now it's time for you to do the same."

Mads's hand still rested on his screen. I could see how the lines on his palm formed paths and valleys. I kept my eyes trained there, afraid I would say more and not wanting to let a rush of emotion call forward what I really wanted to say—*Why do I feel like I can't live without you? Why do I feel like I love you more than I love my children? I wish we could go back to how we were before...when I knew for certain no other woman would ever turn your head.*

"Laney...look at me..."

Mads was peering at me, his gaze steady, those lips I'd kissed and longed to kiss again slightly parted. He placed his right hand on his chest, on his heart. I could already feel my lower lip wobbling. *Hold it together, girl.* Then he bit his lower lip and smiled at me and I couldn't help smiling back. I touched my left hand to the screen, matching my fingertips with his. For a moment I imagined the roughness of his fingertips on mine.

"Laney, I will do anything for you. Anything." Then he lowered his voice. "Do you remember when we first met? How we connected?"

"I can never forget that..."

"It's still there, Laney, that connection...we just have to hold on to it. And I'm not letting go."

* * *

After his call, I couldn't concentrate or relax. I think Freya picked up on my mood because she was also restless. I ended up calling Peyton and asking her if she could babysit Liv so I could go to yoga class again. We were late arriving but the instructor didn't seem to mind. At first I could not even manage to follow along with a simple sun salutation. His voice crept into my mind, distracting me, asking me what I wanted...did I still want him...did I still want our marriage.

"Clear your mind, Laney..." Heaven, our instructor, reminded me. She drifted towards me, placed her hands on my sides and adjusted my position. "Breathe slowly now...remember to center yourself, think of your safe place, exhale...."

Her voice calmed me, smoothing away the rough edges and cocooning me. I could hear my blood rushing through my veins, my breath easing in and out of my lungs. Below me, Freya pushed herself up on her hands, her chubby rump in the air as she tried to balance. She sang "Mama" as she planted her fat little feet on the yoga mat. I followed suit, stretching my body and following all the motions, letting my energy flow. I watched my daughter twist and turn, listened to the unbridled joy in her laughter. She tumbled onto the mat and rolled over on her back. As I held a downward dog, Freya cooed at me and clapped her hands. A laugh bubbled from within me.

My body felt pliant and warm and soothed.

As the class came to an end, I lay on my mat, with Freya cuddling into me. My eyes closed, I continued to let my mind drift as I savored this quiet moment with little girl. I was into my second week of coming to this class and the more I came, the closer I felt to my daughter. After months of sometimes wondering what had happened to my maternal instincts, I finally felt like we'd bonded. I could say I loved her and I felt that love so strongly. I could look at my daughter and feel the love I knew Mads always had for her. Love that I sometimes was afraid I'd faked. But now...with every day I was with her, without worrying as I compared myself to the supermothers who lived in our apartment building, or fretting that my marriage was crumbling before my eyes and trying to balance the attention and affection I gave to both my daughters, I knew without a doubt that I adored Freya.

Heaven led us through the last part of our meditation. The lights were dimmed. I opened my eyes. Sunlight splashed into the room, warming the beech floors and the masonry wall. "Let your mind return to your now...slowly, let all the questions in your heart find their answers...remind yourself of all the love within you."

I breathed out slowly and flexed my fingers and toes. My thoughts filled with an image of Mads, walking ahead of me on the beach, Liv in his arms, the two of them laughing as he splashed in the surf. He stopped and waited for Freya and me to join them. He stretched out his hand and I grabbed it, lacing my fingers with his and letting him pull me to him. I missed the ebb and flow of what was our life.

I missed him.

"I think Mads is coming," I said very carefully as my aunt and I walked home from the yoga studio. "Unless I misunderstood him."

"Is that what you want?" Cecily slid down her sunglasses. I was pretty convinced that my aunt was probably the most glamorous retiree in Juno Beach. In her colorful linen tunic and silk shorts, she looked more like she should be lounging on a terrace with a Bellini rather than pushing her grand-niece's stroller. "Stop picking at your cuticles, my darling."

"I do...want him to come, I mean." I swept my bangs back. The air was sticky and wet. Would it rain again?

"Then you should tell him."

"I have..." I recounted our conversation for her and then added, "He said he still felt a connection between us, that he knew it was still there. We just need to hold on to it."

"He's right," my aunt said. "Some couples, they lose it, let it fritter away. Or they never had it. Your parents, they never had it. I think your mother tried so hard to get your father to feel it..."

We walked for a while without speaking. I hadn't thought about my parents for a long time. Well, I'd thought about my mother. She was often in my thoughts, her voice sometimes guiding me when I felt confused or alone.

"Cecily, did my father ever really love my mother?"

"Darling, I think he tried. But your father..." She shook her head and sighed. We were nearing her neighborhood now, leaving the wide main streets for the narrower tree-lined lanes.

"Where is he now?"

I hadn't seen my father since that awful Thanksgiving in New York. He'd ruined my first Thanksgiving with Liv. He'd tried to force his way into my life again—as though he had a right to do so. His presumption still bothered me. How could he take for granted that he still held a place in my life when he'd abandoned me? How could he even think he had a right to be a part of my children's life? Even Mads's father didn't think it was a given that he would have access to our girls. It had taken months for him to even call and ask if he could meet Liv. It had taken years for Mads and him to finally resume something of a father-son relationship—and there was still tension between them because of how Benjamin had abandoned Mads and his mother.

"Do you really want to know?"

I nodded. "I'm wondering if I should let him into my daughters' lives."

We turned the corner to Dogwood Lane. I could see Peyton and Liv in the front yard with the bubble blower, sending enormous soap bubbles in the air.

"If you're serious about this, I think you should meet him on your own first," Cecily advised.

"Is he still in North Carolina?"

"No...he actually lives here in Florida. He's south of here, in Fort Lauderdale."

"So I could actually drive there..."

"You could. I don't do it often and he's my brother."

"I thought you'd worked through your differences."

"With Lionel, there are always problems. My brother doesn't know how to be happy or appreciate what he has in his life."

Once we were in the yard, Liv dropped her bubble blower and ran over to me. She wrapped her arms around my legs, welcoming me home with a declaration of "Mommy, I love you!"

"I love you too, sweetie."

My aunt smiled at us. "Just think about this—what you have with your girls. Do you want Lionel to affect this? Just think carefully before you let him in again."

From the backseat, Liv was chattering in a combination of Danish and English, still excited from her chat with her father. "Gramma, *papa kommer*! He is taking *min* Bobbi Fox on a *flyvemaskine*!"

"English, Liv. Gramma doesn't speak Danish," I reminded her.

"What is she saying?"

"She said her father is coming, and he's bringing her stuffed fox on an airplane."

"Smart boy." My aunt nodded as she drove. "I knew he'd come to his senses."

"So you think he's coming?"

"Of course he is, honey. He misses you. He misses his daughters. He wants his family back."

CHAPTER TWELVE: Mads

Welcome to America

Once I'd checked in and gone through security, I avoided the duty free shop and found a quiet spot where I could try to collect my thoughts. I hated flying. Short flights were okay; by the time restlessness set off too many triggers in me, it was time to land. But long flights were a chore. It was one of the reasons I never flew alone. The last long-haul flight I took was when Laney and I flew to Mallorca—and even that wasn't very long of a flight. But four hours on a plane and too much anxiety and turbulence had worn me out. I'd contrived too many worst-case scenarios in my head. I fidgeted and shifted in my seat until Laney clasped my hand and massaged my knuckles with her thumb. She was pregnant with Freya then...already in her fifth month and we knew this was probably our last vacation until she was born. And Laney distracted me with idle talk about baby names.

"Should we name her Monika?" she'd wondered when even her touch did little to calm me down. "Or Josefina."

"What?" I cast a nervous glance at the window. Laney reached across me and drew down the sun shade.

"What should we name our daughter?" Gently, she pulled my hand over to her baby bump, barely noticeable under the tunic she wore, but as soon as she covered my hand and held it there, the white noise of my nerves ebbed. "I know we don't know if it's a boy or a girl...but it *feels* like it's a girl again."

She knew me so well. She knew when I needed to be soothed; she sensed when my desire for her was driving me crazy, even before I reached for her. Sometimes I was certain she could read my mind. During that flight, Laney distracted me, never letting me give in to my fear of flying, her voice a drug for me as she rambled off different names, asked me which sounded nicer as she said them. I barely noticed when the plane touched down in Palma. I was so happy we'd decided on a name for the little girl who was waiting patiently to be born.

I'd have to distract myself this time. At least I'd remembered to pack my iPad and the John le Carré novel Laney had given me at the beginning of the summer. I checked my watch for the umpteenth time. I still had around two hours until my flight would board. A few meters away from me a trio of teenage boys tried to order beers from the sports bar. The female bartender shook her head no and offered them sodas instead. They took it in stride, struggling and laughing as they accepted the three bottles of Coke she set before them. Henrik and I had tried the same thing the first time we went away on our own. We were going to island-hop in Greece and we thought no one would notice how wet behind the ears we were. We failed at getting beers too and had to settle for orange Fanta. I wondered if it would be the same for Freya and Liv when they were old enough to travel on their own.

Thinking of my two girls reminded me of my traveling companion, Bobbi Fox. Laney had made the fox while she was pregnant with Liv. She'd found some patterns online and, with Ingrid's help, sewed a menagerie of stuffed woodland animals for the nursery. From the moment we brought Liv home, though, the only one she had eyes for was the scarlet fox with its blue and white gingham bandana. Bobbi Fox kept nightmares at bay, distracted Liv when a temper tantrum threatened to flare, elicited excited laughter when Liv was bored. I could only wonder how Laney had got Liv through these weeks without Bobbi Fox.

In roughly ten hours, I would be on American soil, I'd be with my family again. I thought back to that day in Humlebæk, when I'd bumped into my father. He'd tried to warn me and I'd missed all the signs. He'd looked out for my wife and children when I let my work get in the way. But now, I was going to make things right.

Ten hours. I could handle it. As long as at the end of it, I would see my wife again, hold my children again. I could do this.

When they announced my flight, I sent a text message to Cecily: "I'm on my way."

Her reply came just as I was boarding: "It's about time."

Somehow I managed to fall asleep during takeoff. I dreamt of my mother, as she was before the accident. In the dream we were walking along the beach in winter. Snow dusted the sand and a milky mist hung over the water. My mother held a sleeping Freya as she imparted words of wisdom to me. But the me in the dream was a younger, angrier version of me. And when she tried to give Freya to me, I wouldn't take her. My mother forced me to take her. "This is your daughter," she reminded me. "You helped create her, so you need to help love her as well." When I finally reached for her, Freya disintegrated into dust. I cried out and demanded to know what my mother had done to her.

"I haven't done anything, Mads. This is what happens when love is gone."

I jerked awake to the plane bumping through the clouds.

"Ladies and gentlemen, please return to your seats and fasten your seatbelt. We're experiencing a bit of turbulence."

The woman sitting beside me glanced my way but I wouldn't make eye contact with her. She'd been eying me since we boarded the flight. I checked my seatbelt was fastened and pulled out my iPad. I'd recorded some of the FaceTime chats I'd had with the girls. Their laughter and smiling faces would keep me from thinking about how the plane was being knocked around by turbulence.

Laney's face filled the screen. She was focused on keyboard. Her dark hair was pulled back in a loose ponytail. This was the last FaceTime chat we'd had. The only one without the kids. She'd called me in the middle of the night. I'd heard my iPad ping and when I'd fumbled for it, she was there, her face scrubbed clean of makeup, her lips parted as though she were about to speak.

"Did I wake you...?" she'd asked though she knew what time it was in Copenhagen. She was wearing a tank top and one strap was sliding off her shoulder. "I know it's late there."

My own reply was muffled. It didn't matter what I'd said. I forgot everything as I fumbled for my headphones, tuned out everyone around me and immersed myself in my wife's voice. She licked her lips, lowered her eyes so her lashes fanned her cheeks. She was so lovely...how stupid I was, letting her slip away from me. We talked as we hadn't for so long. About how we felt, about where we were going...I asked her if she was leaving me for good. She hesitated, then said no. "I needed a break...I think you needed one from me too."

I replayed one part of the chat...when Laney swept her ponytail over her right shoulder and turned her head to speak to Liv. The elegant line of her neck mesmerized me. I'd kissed her there so many times, nuzzled into her and breathed in the scent of her skin. When she'd turned back to the screen, she seemed surprised I'd waited. Then she touched her fingers to the screen and said, "I wish I could touch you again. I miss you, Mads."

"I'll come," I'd told her. "If you want me there, I'll come."

"Then come."

The woman beside me cleared her throat several times. I kept my eyes trained on my iPad screen. Why couldn't she leave me alone? The last thing I wanted to do was make idle small talk with her. I'd switched now from the recorded FaceTime chats to my photo albums. Thumbnails of images from our wedding lined the screen. Whenever I looked at these photographs, it took me back four years ago to that July day in an instant. All of the craziness that preceded it—the mix-up with venues, the dress Laney ordered from the US that never arrived...Henrik nearly losing our wedding rings. None of it mattered. We walked down the aisle together since neither of us wanted to be given away. "I'm not property," Laney had said from the very beginning. "I am giving myself to you and you're giving yourself to me."

Marius, Laney's colleague, took most of the photos. He spent most of our wedding ceremony and reception on his feet, wandering around the church and then the park where we'd had our reception dinner, capturing candid moments and spontaneous shots. Nearly every picture was perfect. One in particular was my favorite: Marius had managed to catch us as we danced and Laney was laughing at something I'd said. Her head was tipped back, and the white flowers in her hair looked as though they'd bloomed just for her. My hands rested on the curve of her hips and it was obvious there was nowhere else I wanted to be, no one else I wanted to have. Henrik used to tease me and say I was too intense with Laney, that it was a wonder I didn't scare her off with the intensity of my love for her. In that picture, I looked as though I would devour her with my desire for her. I was gazing at her and only her. I think in that moment I was wondering how much longer we had to stay...when could we escape to the hotel room we'd booked as our honeymoon suite, so that I could undo each of the tiny buttons on her dress and watch it fall away from her body. I was addicted to the gentle hum of her body, of the song it sang just for me.

"Those are gorgeous pictures." The woman in the aisle seat gripped my arm. She'd angled her body toward me. "Did you take them?"

I shook her hand off my arm. "They're from my wedding."

"Well, it looks as though you had a lovely ceremony."

She was smiling a little too brightly. I recognized that look from my sperm donor days, the look of someone who wanted more than you could ever give them. I didn't want her to think any conversation was encouragement or mutual interest. I didn't return her smile. I nodded absently and turned my face toward the window. The sky was still blue, sunset still a long way off. On the in-flight entertainment screen, the map showed that we were somewhere over Greenland. Soon we'd enter North American airspace.

The hours were ticking down. I wondered how Laney would react to my arrival. I want her to be happy to see me; I wanted her to forgive me for being such a fucking stupid idiot. I squeezed my thumb in my fist and let the words repeat in my head: *"I will do anything for you, I don't ever want to be without you again, take me back...please...take me back."*

By the time we landed, my seatmate had finally given up trying to ensnare me in conversation and turned her attentions to the man in the other aisle seat. I collected my belongings, tried to still my nerves and remind myself that she wanted me to come. I just had to hope we both wanted the same thing. And if she'd decided she wanted to take another route...maybe I could persuade her to change her mind.

Getting through passport control took a hell of a lot longer than I remembered. After what felt like an eternity, it was my turn to approach one of the windows. The woman who interviewed me was so stern and emotionless at first. She tapped on her computer, then looked up. "Are you travelling alone?"

I nodded, scratched my chin and said, "My wife is already here. She came a few weeks ago with our daughters."

"And your wife is American?"

"Yeah, she is. Well, she has dual citizenship. American and Danish."

"And where are you staying while you're here?"

"With her aunt, in Juno Beach." I rested both of my hands on the counter. My nerves were flaring up again. My hands shook a little. She glanced at them, then started typing again. That's when I blurted out, "She left me... I took her for granted, I was stupid and she left me. So I've come to work things out."

"So you're here for pleasure, then?" She tried to keep a straight face in spite of my perhaps ill-timed confession. Then she flashed a smile at me and added, "I hope it works out. I always root for love." Then she stamped my passport. "Welcome to America, Mr. Rasmussen. And good luck."

CHAPTER THIRTEEN: Laney

And I Love Him

"Today is almost the best day ever," Liv announced in Danish. Her head rested on my shoulder as I carried her. We'd gone to the beach together with Rebecca and Lorelei to collect shells. Now we had a sack full of mother-of-pearl shells and pebbles. My aunt had taken Freya on an outing of her own. She thought Freya might enjoy a trip to the Fort Lauderdale Zoological Gardens instead.

"I'm glad you think so," I told her. "I want you to have fun while we're here."

Beside us, Rebecca and Lorelei were singing as they skipped and danced their way up Dogwood Lane. Hanging out with them, seeing a different way of interacting with my daughters and not having to feel like it was all a competition to be supermom was refreshing. I liked how Rebecca and her daughters had fun together—she let them be kids, she didn't care about dressing them up like little fashion plates or turning them into mini-adults. If they wanted to wear torn jeans and T-shirts and blow bubbles on the beach, she was okay with that. I had to hold onto this when I went back to Copenhagen—I didn't have to compete with the other mothers, I could be me and that was fine.

"Thanks so much for suggesting this outing, Rebecca." We'd come to a stop outside of her bungalow. "This was exactly what Liv and I needed."

"Honey, you're so welcome—and we were glad for the company." She let go of Lorelei's hand. As soon as she did, Lorelei took off across the yard and did a handstand.

"I was wondering...would you be able to go somewhere with me tomorrow?" I shifted Liv in my arms. She was humming against my neck. "I need to go to Fort Lauderdale and I don't really want to go on my own."

"I have to work until 1PM, but I'm free after that," she said. "So...what's the mission? Are we shopping...or are you looking for a place here?"

"What? Oh, no...I'll have to go back to Denmark soon. Sooner or later, I'll have to work things out with my husband...and I want to, and I think he wants it too." I bounced Liv in my arms. "Cecily told me my father's living here in Florida now...and I haven't seen him since Liv was a baby. I just don't want to go alone."

"Difficult situation?"

"You could say that..."

"Yeah, sure, count me in. I can swing by as soon as I am done. Peyton and Lorelei are going on an excursion with Cecily and Heaven tomorrow."

"Is it the art museum trip she mentioned this morning?"

"Yes, they do this every summer for the kids who come to the yoga classes," Rebecca said. "Are Liv and Freya going too?"

I nodded. "Cecily thought it would be fun for them."

"So, then we leave as soon as I am done at the studio. And we take a road trip to Fort Lauderdale."

"Thanks for agreeing to this."

"No problem. I know what it's like having bad blood with family. I hope you and your father will be able to resolve your differences..."

We said our goodbyes, then Liv and I continued down the road to my aunt's house. I didn't recognize the car parked behind my aunt's in the driveway. On closer inspection, I saw it was a rental car.

Liv mumbled to me that she was hungry. "We'll have a snack as soon as we've freshened up," I told her. "Grilled cheese sandwiches?"

She shook her head. "Mango...I like mangoes."

"Mangoes it will be, then," I agreed. I managed to open the door. I could hear my aunt in the kitchen talking to someone. I thought perhaps she was on the phone with Eddy. But then I heard a male voice...a voice I recognized. I stopped in my tracks. Liv, so attuned to anything connected with her father, reacted immediately.

"Papa!" she squirmed out of my arms and ran into the kitchen, still singing "Papa" until she found him.

I found the courage to move again. He'd caught Liv in his arms and was giving her a tight hug. I wanted to run to him, to cast myself at him, but I held back. He needed this moment with Liv and she needed it too. My aunt was beaming at their reunion.

"*Papa, du er her endelig!*" Liv giggled as she planted wet kisses on his cheeks. "*Jeg savnede dig!*"

"I missed you too, sweetheart," Mads admitted. He cradled Liv's face in one hand and smiled at her. "I missed you so much I couldn't wait any longer to see you."

I set the bag of shells down on the floor and joined them in the kitchen. The air crackled with our mutual longing and tension. We both wanted to banish this distance between us, yet we were afraid of taking the next step. So much had happened.

I tried to smile but it wavered... I felt suddenly shy and uncertain. Mads looked as insecure as I felt. We both smiled but didn't make a move. "Hi..." God, what a stupid way to greet him when we hadn't seen one another in so long. I raised my hand in a wave then let my hand drop to my side.

"Hi...so...I came." He smiled at me over the top of Liv's head. His neck and ears flushed red. They always did when he was nervous.

"Yeah, you did, didn't you?"

We both laughed nervously.

Liv gave us both a quizzical look. "Mommy, aren't you going to hug Papa?" she demanded.

"I will, sweetie," I assured her. "I just wanted you to have a good welcome with Daddy."

She gave him an extra squeeze. "Freya will be happy Papa is here too. Did you bring Bobbi Fox?"

Mads nodded. "I did—she's waiting for you in your room."

"She missed me—didn't she?"

"Of course she did, *lille ven*. She said she couldn't sleep without you."

"Me neither! But Mommy told me Bobbi Fox adventures!"

"She did? I'll bet they were exciting." Though he was talking to Liv, Mads's eyes were trained on me. The intensity of his gaze made me wish we were alone. Even with everything we needed to work through, the pull to be close to him, to feel his strength and warmth never left me. I wanted so badly to nuzzle into him, feel his razor stubble scrape my cheeks, to feel his hands taking possession of me. But I waited patiently. I had to. As much as I wanted him, my daughter needed this time with her father.

Instead, I turned to my aunt and said, "This is a nice surprise."

"It certainly is," she agreed. But the satisfied expression on her face told me she'd known all along that he was coming. She'd probably spoken to Mads more often than I had to ensure he understood that he needed to come to bring us back together. I should have been annoyed, but I couldn't erase the silly grin from my face.

Mads pressed several kisses to Liv's cheek then finally set her down on the floor. She squealed with delight and ran past him, already longing to be reunited with Bobbi Fox. My aunt followed suit, knowing we needed this time alone.

We both stood there, the distance between us pulsating.

Then he crossed the room and grabbed me and I gasped in his arms. I held him close and didn't let go. Oh God...he was finally here. Even if there was still so much we needed to sort out...he was here, and he was holding me like I was the only woman he'd ever wanted. Being in his arms again, feeling his warmth and the security of him...I was home again. And when I realized he was sobbing, his body trembling against mine, I held him tighter and stroked his neck.

"Don't ever leave me again, Laney...please...not like this again."

I didn't answer, I just held him tighter. There was no one else who mattered more to me than the man in my arms.

* * *

Once Freya woke from her nap and realized her father was with us, she and Liv claimed him as theirs. In a way, this was the best solution. We needed this...they needed his attention, and Mads gave it freely. Even though he looked exhausted from the flight—and I knew how tense he was during long-haul flights—he gave them his undivided attention, cuddling Freya, listening to Liv as she babbled to him about how good it was to have him and Bobbi Fox there. I hovered for a while in the doorway to the girls' room, my arms folded across my chest as I watched him together with our girls. It hurt to think that I'd deprived him of this—no matter how much I'd needed this time, I saw how hard it had been for him. I backed away from the room and retreated to my aunt's garden. Outside, the air was wet and thick and heavy. Soon it would probably rain—another afternoon thunderstorm.

I sank into one of the porch chairs and let out a long sigh. My hands were shaking. I tried yoga breathing to calm down but still it didn't help. I didn't know what to do. He was here; I wanted to be near him, I didn't trust myself near him. It was a relief when Aunt Cecily came out and joined me. She claimed the chair by mine and said, "The girls are over the moon he's here."

"I'm glad. They missed him."

"You did too, Laney," Cecily took my hand and squeezed it. "It's okay to admit it."

"Did you know he was coming?"

"Eddy told me when he'd booked his ticket."

"She should have told me..."

"Would it have made a difference?" She stroked my hair with her other hand. "My darling, you missed him. You told me you wanted to work through things with him. And now he's here."

Being here with my aunt made me wish my mother were also here. I knew my mother would tell me to work things through with Mads. Even when my father had been at his worst, she tried to talk things out with him in her calm, collected way. She didn't give in to shouting or throwing things—even when she was losing her patience.

My aunt's voice stayed calm as she spoke to me. "Remember the guided meditation you've learned, remember what you've told me during our evening chats. You want your marriage to work. And Mads wants the same thing. So when the girls have finally let go of him, you two need to talk...about anything, about everything."

"I do want my marriage to work..."

"I want that too, Laney." Mads's voice startled me. I turned quickly. He stood in the doorway, his hands in his pockets. "I haven't given up on us. I hope you haven't either."

"Mads, are you hungry?" My aunt asked. She let go of my hand and stood. "I'm sure that airline food was appalling."

He grinned at my aunt. "It was pretty disgusting. But I'm spoiled...Laney is such a good cook."

My aunt patted his cheek as she passed him. "I'll go and start dinner. You and Laney need some time together."

So we were alone again, neither of us moved at first. Thunder rumbled in the sky. The air around us charged with electricity...or was it the tension between us, building after these weeks apart?

"There are so many things I want to say to you," he started. "I don't even know where I should begin...I'm sorry. I'm so sorry about everything."

Mads took another step towards me. I wanted to say I was sorry as well but the words were stuck in my chest. He swiped his hand over his mouth and glanced away. His jaw tensed.

I wanted to reach out and stroke away that tension. I knew he wouldn't stop me, but I didn't trust myself not to take things further. But...I stood, I went to him and touched him. I had to... He didn't move...though I heard his breath catch in his throat. He wanted this too. His arms came around me and pulled me closer. I leaned my head on his shoulder and breathed in the scent of him. "I don't know what to do, Laney..." he breathed in my ear. "I don't know what I should do to make you trust me again, to believe in me again."

He kissed me then...first pressing a soft kiss on my forehead...my lips parted in anticipation as he tipped my head back, brushed his lips over my cheeks...the tip of my nose and then finally my lips. His breath was hot; I wanted to kiss him forever. I slid my hands under his shirt, anxious to feel his bare skin again. We stood like this, kissing tentatively then letting our kisses grow deeper, more passionate, until a clap of thunder startled us.

"Maybe we should go inside," I ventured. The sky had darkened...the air was so thick with humidity it felt like droplets of rain were already falling. Mads trailed his fingertips along my cheeks, then he dipped in for another kiss. I moaned against his lips, pressed my body closer to his.

"I know we have a lot to talk about," Mads said softly. "But tonight...I just want to lie beside you again. I just want to be near you."

"I want that too." I captured his lips again, savoring the taste of him, how he knew exactly how to hold me, to kiss me back.

"So...tomorrow...we start from scratch?" Fat droplets of rain finally began to fall, pelting the dry soil and the porch railing. Mads shielded me from it, turning us so the rain hit his back. Heat rose from his body, seeping into my clothing, drenching me with his scent. I loved the smell of him, loved how safe it felt to be in his arms.

I nodded. "Tomorrow, we can talk about everything."

CHAPTER FOURTEEN: Mads

This Is Love

I woke slowly, absorbing the sounds around me, stretching and trying to gauge what time it actually was. My limbs creaked with each movement—was it the aftermath of a long flight or another sign I was getting older? Maybe both.

"Papa..." I opened my eyes and turned my head toward my daughter. She scrambled onto the bed and lay down beside me. She smelled freshly bathed. Her newly washed curls were still damp. "Mommy's gone for a walk. She said I was to wake you."

"I'm glad you did," I told her. I gave her nose a playful tap. "Where's Freya?"

"Mommy took her for a walk too."

"But you didn't want to go?"

Liv shook her head. "I want to stay with you so you won't be lonely." She patted the top of my head with one hand while she clutched her fox to her with the other hand.

Her skin was so tan now, like an acorn. Her dark, coppery eyes reminded me of Laney's. Laney swore her eyes were simply brown, but I saw the flecks of bronze and copper. And when her face was turned to the sun, her eyes flared amber and mesmerized me. Liv's eyes were the same. She was going to be a heartbreaker when she was older. I had the feeling Laney and I would have lots of headaches in our future thanks to our daughter and the boys whose hearts she'd break. But for now I was glad she was still four years old and the only thing she cared about was her stuffed fox and whether we'd spend the day at the playground.

"Will you sleep all day, Papa?"

"No...I need to get up, I need to take a shower."

"Mommy said you snored last night."

"I don't snore."

"Yes, you do, Papa. You sound like an airplane when you snore." And then she imitated what I apparently sounded like when I snored. She giggled and the sound of it filled me with happiness. Liv thrust Bobbi Fox at me and demanded I kiss her. "Bobbi Fox needs love too. She doesn't have a papa."

I indulged my little girl and kissed her fox. "Papa needs breakfast now. And a shower."

"I can make you breakfast, Papa."

"No, it's okay, *lille ven*, I'll make breakfast, but you and Bobbi can keep me company. Okay?"

She nodded enthusiastically and scrambled off the bed. "Come on, Papa. No more bed."

I trudged out of bed, grabbed a T-shirt from where I'd tossed it last night. My body still felt thick and heavy from the flight. In the kitchen, Liv was already trying to pull a chair over to the counter. I directed her back over the table and took over fixing breakfast. I settled for making scrambled eggs and toast along with a pot of coffee while Liv entertained me with Bobbi Fox stories. At some point, while I dazed out over my eggs, Cecily arrived from a morning at the studio. She gave my shoulder a warm squeeze and then joined me for a cup of coffee. Liv was still chattering, now doing voices for Bobbi Fox too.

Cecily cocked her eyebrows at Liv's story. "Have you been talking your papa's ears off?"

Liv shook her head. "Papa is listening."

"I always listen," I assured her, but my head felt cottony and my body was craving a few more hours of sleep.

"You look like you could do with a long shower and more R & R." Cecily surmised.

"R & R?"

"Rest and relaxation. That's what the GIs used to call it—R & R."

"Yeah, I could do with that, but a little bird thought it was time for me to wake up."

"It was time, Papa." Liv pouted at me. "You sleep all day. Then you keep Mommy up all night. Mommy needs sleep too."

I think I must have blushed. My skin felt hot and Cecily was covering her mouth, trying not to laugh.

"You think I keep Mommy awake?"

Liv nodded. "You do, Papa. I hear her. You talk a lot, and you make funny noises."

I couldn't hold it in anymore. Neither could Cecily. We both broke down laughing while Liv gave us concerned looks. She slid out of her chair and announced that she and Bobbi Fox were going to play in the garden.

"That daughter of yours is a mess, Mads Rasmussen." Cecily was still trying to contain her laughter. "Well, at least she knows her father keeps her mother entertained."

"I didn't think they could hear us... I thought we were pretty quiet."

"Hmm...no, well. You're not but you try." Cecily mused. "You were quiet last night, but I remember when I was in Copenhagen for your wedding and I spent the night in your guest room. Well, I know you make Laney happy..." She laughed again.

"I try. Lately I failed at it, but I want to change that." I went over to the door to the garden to check on Liv. She was sitting on the porch steps, talking to Bobbi Fox.

Cecily came over and stood beside me. She touched my shoulder again. "Now that you're here, you and Laney can begin working together on what you want."

"Liv said she went for a walk?"

"She goes every morning. She meditates while she walks. It does her a world of good." Cecily stepped out on the back porch, then turned and added, "Maybe you should join her tomorrow."

"I don't want to intrude on it, though, if it's something she needs for herself."

"Mads, maybe you both need it," Cecily countered. "You've both avoided talking about the problems you've had. And when she's walking on the beach, she's thinking through what she wants and what has gone wrong and how to fix it."

I let Cecily's words sink in while I watched Liv stretch out her hand to catch a butterfly. She sat very still, her fingers barely twitching. It didn't take long before a monarch butterfly landed on her index finger. I held my breath, wondering how long it would rest there or if Liv's contained excitement would scare it away. She sensed this was a special moment. She didn't giggle, didn't call out for me or try to capture the butterfly. Instead she bent forward a bit and peered at the butterfly's wings.

"You need to treasure my niece, Mads. You need to hold her dear."

"I do, Cecily. Trust me, I do."

"She gave you two very sweet little girls...she gave you the family you said you always wanted. That's proof of her love for you. You treasure her, and you and I will be fine."

I'd showered and dressed by the time Laney came home from her walk. Liv and I were in the garden, searching for more butterflies. She was convinced there were millions of them in the bushes, though we'd only seen one so far.

Laney latched the gate behind her and then pushed the stroller up the path towards us. She'd swept her hair into a messy bun, showing off the lovely curve of her neck. Her skin glistened there. If I held her, she'd smell of sunlight, heat and something more—something that I always connected with her. Freya was strapped in the stroller, the brim of her cotton sunhat drooping over her face. She must have fallen asleep on the way home.

"It's so hot today," Laney said and swiped beads of perspiration from her neck. "I think I need another shower."

"I may have to help you, then..." I said with a grin. A smile flickered over her lips. She lowered her eyes and then looked up at me through the veil of her lashes.

"Mads...the kids..."

"Freya can't understand everything we say and Liv's too busy looking for butterfly nests." We were speaking English together, the language we'd fallen in love in. Sometimes we behaved as though it was our secret language since Liv didn't always understand when we spoke took quickly, but her English was so good now that we couldn't depend on it as our code for much longer.

"Is Cecily still here?"

"She's still inside. She was waiting for you so she could take the girls on an excursion?" At least, that's what I thought Cecily had told me. Jet lag still fogged my brain. I just knew I wanted some time with Laney.

Once we were alone, I had to remind myself that we couldn't ignore the problems that had led to Laney leaving me. It was too easy to push it aside, to coax her into kissing me or to slide one hand along her side and enjoy the sensation of our bodies coming together. So we sat on the porch swing and tried to address some of our issues. Laney hugged her knees to her chest. She watched me from under her fringe. I reached out my hand, brushed her hair away from her eyes. I wanted to see them, didn't want her to hide behind her hair.

"Did you sleep with her?" Somehow I'd known she would ask this first. She spoke so softly I nearly missed it. "I know I shouldn't care. I should just want us to move forward...but I need to know."

My hand trailed down her neck. I needed to feel her, even if it was simply a fleeting touch. "I never slept with her, Laney. I didn't want her...not like that."

"But you were attracted to her, weren't you?"

"I don't know...yes, I was. I thought she was sexy."

"I knew it..." She let out a long sigh. "I saw how you looked at her. "

We sat there...the specter of Benny between us.

"She kissed me."

"I know she did. I saw the evidence..."

"No, she kissed me again...she thought I wanted it, but I didn't. And I told her. I told her I wasn't interested in her." Laney's shoulders tensed, but I didn't let go. I needed her to know that she was the only one I wanted in my life—no matter how stupid and thoughtless I'd been. "I think I just liked that she was paying attention to me. It sounds stupid. I kept telling myself her flirting was harmless, that she wasn't interested in me like that. And then it felt like you were pulling away."

"She kissed you..."

"I don't want her though. I never did. I'm here with you because you're who I want, Laney."

Laney drew back but I caught her hand before she could move too far away.

"I want to be honest with you, Laney. I don't want us to have any secrets. I'm telling you this because I know we drifted apart, but the thing is...I don't want anyone else. I don't want to *be* with anyone else. Just you."

"So what do we do now?"

"Laney, you can't tell me you were never attracted to anyone else. Even while we've been together. You never looked at another man and wondered?"

"I don't know, Mads. Honestly? I've been so busy with Liv and Freya—"

"Don't use the kids as a buffer. Let's just be honest."

"I don't know. I probably looked at some guy and thought he was good-looking...but I never acted on it."

"Neither did I."

"You flirted with her, and she was flirting with you. You forgot about me because of her."

Neither of us spoke for a while. Laney pressed her lips together. What was she thinking? I hoped she wasn't imagining the worst. I wanted to reassure her, but nothing seemed right.

"One night, I heard you on the phone, laughing..." I could still remember that night. I'd fallen asleep while reading to Liv and woken up from Laney's laughter. "I don't know who you were talking to that night. Maybe it was Jesper. Maybe it was Ingrid or Niklas. But you sounded the way you used to...and when you hung up, all that light and sparkle was gone. And I knew it was my fault."

"I thought you'd stopped loving me... We were barely sleeping together, it felt like you were avoiding being with me." Her words came out in small bursts. She kept her eyes cast down, but the uncertainty in her voice came through. "I thought you'd realized this wasn't the life you wanted. Like maybe all of this between us happened too fast and now finally the reality was setting in—"

"No, this is the life I want." I pulled her closer. I needed her near me.

"All the arguments...all those nights when you barely touched me...sometimes days went by without us even really speaking to one another."

"Laney...last night...did it feel like I wanted anyone else?"

She shook her head. "It was the same for me. Sometimes I wonder how it is that I love you so much that no one else matters."

"There is no one else for me, Laney. I don't want to spend my life with anyone else."

Of course my phone rang. Of course it was Anton. Laney glanced at my phone display. "You should probably answer it. It could be an emergency."

"It can wait."

"Mads, go ahead. Answer. It's okay."

When I answered, she pushed off the porch swing and then walked down the porch steps. As she crossed the yard, I watched the sway of her hips. She glanced over her shoulder at me. There was a double sun lounger in the shade of the tree at the back of the garden. She settled there, easing her feet out of her flip-flops. And I watched...not paying very much attention to Anton as I took in how truly lovely my wife was.

"Sorry about that...it was Anton, he just wanted to tell me how the forum was going." I pressed the power button on my phone and turned it off. "Off now."

"It's okay. I can't expect you to completely forget about your business."

I joined her on the sun lounger now. Laney shaded her eyes with her hand. "I have to go soon," she said.

"Where? I thought we had all day..."

"I'm actually going to see my dad...I don't know if it's worth it, but I thought I should try."

This was big. After everything he'd put her through, she'd sworn she never wanted him in her life again. "Do you want me to go with you?"

"No, you're probably still exhausted. And I already asked Rebecca to go with me."

"Who's Rebecca?"

"She's a new friend." And then she told me about Rebecca while I tried to distract her with caresses. I couldn't help it. After weeks of not being near her, I needed the reassurance that she was still with me, that she wouldn't simply slip away and vanish from my life completely. "She's helped me a lot since I've been here. She's got two daughters and she's been raising them on her own..."

"Sounds like you look up to her." I was glad she'd opened up and let a new friend in. Our small circle of friends in Copenhagen sometimes felt claustrophobic. We rarely let new people into our bubble. Laney had often said she didn't need new girlfriends when she had Eddy and Ingrid, and I had the guys from the workshop and Henrik. Adam too, though we didn't see each other as often as before. But Laney had needed someone else even without knowing it. And when she opened up and shared Rebecca's story with me, I understood why.

"She's strong...and I love how easy she is with her daughters, even when they're driving her insane." She turned on her side so we could face one another. "Watching how she is with her girls made me realize how I was taking a lot of things too seriously. She told me I should calm down, just accept that I can't do or control everything. "

"We'd go crazy if we tried."

"You don't try to control everything...I should have realized that. You have that same easiness with Liv and Freya. And all this time, I was angry at you because I thought you were just leaving all of the hard stuff to me—"

"I haven't been a good husband. I should have been better at seeing you needed my help, that I was letting you take on too much of the responsibility for our lives." It still bothered me that I'd been so blind to her needs. It didn't matter that I'd thought I was doing the right thing by trying to be successful. "I thought if I could just sell more of my designs...I could give you what you used to have."

"What do you mean?"

"When you were with Niklas—"

"Mads, I don't want what I had with Niklas. If I'd wanted that, I would have stayed with him. I have what I want with you."

"But you never had to worry about the bills being paid, you never had to think twice about if there was enough money for a vacation or to treat yourself to something you wanted. The cleaning service... And I haven't been able to give you and the girls that sort of security."

"Mads, are you crazy?" She grinned at me. "You have given me a home, a family...that's what I always wanted. The expensive vacations? I don't give a shit about that. I love the life we have together. I don't want my husband to disappear into this 'get rich or die trying' mania just because you think I miss having Niklas's money."

"I just want us to have a good life."

"We do have a good life. And it will be better when you stop working so hard and spend more time with us." She stroked my chest through my T-shirt. Her fingertips sent shivers through me. "And we have Liv and Freya...and I want them to have their father...they love being around you, and when you're not there... they ask for you all the time. I can't give them everything. They need you too."

"I just didn't want us to...want for anything. I wanted to show you I could provide for us."

"You already do. You don't have to compete with what you think I miss." She pulled me to her and kissed me gently. "I don't miss my life with Niklas. All I want is you. That's it. Just you."

For a little while, we got a bit lost in one another. I didn't want to let go of her. She didn't want me to. It reminded me of when we first met—how sometimes we could be so focused on one another that the world around us didn't exist. A look could say so much, a touch could lead to a thousand more, a kiss could ignite something akin to wildfire. I think we could have pushed things further...but then Rebecca arrived.

She cleared her throat and said, "Sorry to interrupt."

We sprang apart like guilty teenagers. Laney laughed and adjusted her top. I tried to shield the evidence that I wanted my wife far too much.

"I could come back later," she grinned at us. "I mean, I'm guessing this is Mads, so you probably have a lot to...talk about."

Laney laughed. "We'll pick up where we left off later..."

We most definitely would.

CHAPTER FIFTEEN: Laney

Fathers & Daughters

"Wow! So that was the infamous Mads," Rebecca joked as we drove along the A1A. She tapped her thumbs on the steering wheel. "Why am I not surprised that he's gorgeous? Are all the Danes that good-looking?"

"Some are," I said with a shrug. Having him here still felt so unreal. Even this morning, after waking up beside him, a little shiver went through me—he was here, he still wanted our marriage to work, he'd put me and the kids before his projects and his pursuit of success. I'd lain there watching him sleep, daring every now and then to skim my fingertips over his shorn hair, his strong jaw. He was here. And he still loved me. "I'd introduce you to his cousin, but he's in love with Eddy."

"See? All the good ones are taken. Story of my life." Becks winked at me. "When did he arrive?"

"Yesterday...I think Cecily knew he was coming. She didn't seem at all surprised to see him."

"Ah, she knew then." Becks shook her head and let out a little laugh. "She said something about having a surprise visitor, but I thought she meant Eddy was coming. How does it feel now? Having him here?"

"Honestly? Weird...but good. I missed him, I didn't want to consider that this separation might be permanent. I guess I was hoping he'd come." I fidgeted with the radio until Becks slapped my hand away.

"My car, my radio stations," she teased, then she pressed the tuner button a few times until we settled on a Top 40 radio station. "But if Justin Bieber comes on, please turn the station ASAP...or my head might explode."

We were in luck: Beyoncé's latest single filled the car, saving us—at least for a while—from the horrors of Justin Bieber. As we drove, my thoughts drifted to our destination and why we were going there. Mads's arrival had distracted me enough from even thinking about what I would say to my father. I'd called him yesterday, before Mads's arrival, and told him I thought we needed to clear the air. I'd hoped he would sound at least pleased that I was taking this step, but he'd let out what sounded like a resigned sigh and said, "Come by after lunch. I have a doctor's appointment in the morning." It wasn't the most encouraging or inspiring prelude to any sort of reunion.

"Are you nervous?" Becks adjusted her sunglasses. I reached for mine from the dashboard.

"I don't know what to expect." I admitted. "I don't know if this will lead to anything. I'm not even sure I want him in my daughters' lives..."

I filled Becks in on how my father had treated my mother. Just talking about it still left me hollow. I hoped my daughters would never have to live through anything like it. And I wanted to give my father the benefit of the doubt. If Mads's father could change, then I hoped Lionel could also change. Benjamin was so good with the girls—he'd been so reticent at first, but from the moment he laid eyes on Liv and held her for the first time, he'd begun making an effort to repair his fractured relationship with Mads. Though they were still careful with one another, Benjamin and Mads at least had the sort of father-son relationship where they spoke to one another and sometimes met for coffee. I was probably closer to Benjamin than Mads. I called him often and arranged visits so he and the girls could spend time together. I'd told Benjamin from the start that we wanted him to know his grandchildren, but not if he put drinking above them. And he began changing his ways. When he was with us, he drank alcohol-free beer, juice or seltzer water. When he was in the city, he stopped by and spent time with Liv and Freya. I wanted to give Lionel the same opportunity, even if a tiny part of me was certain he'd squander it.

My father lived in one of those gated communities you always read about or see on TV. We had to sign in at the gate and then follow a curving lane that took us past tidy brick houses that all looked identical. The only thing that differentiated any of the houses was the type of flag hanging from the wall-mounted flag posts. My father had told me to look for the house with the Philadelphia Eagles flag. It wasn't hard to find—all the other houses had flags of smiling suns, bumblebees and happy flowers. But my father—in the midst of Miami Dolphin territory—dared to wave an Eagles flag. It was pretty badass of him; it even made me smile. He'd always been adamant that he would always be an Eagles fan—he'd even cheered for them during the low points. Well, at least he was loyal to something.

We parked outside his house. His car was in the driveway, so we knew he was home. I hesitated getting out of the car, though.

"Hon, do you want me to go in with you?" Rebecca touched my shoulder. I was still staring at the front door of my father's house.

I shook my head. "I need to do this on my own." I pushed open the door. "Will you come back for me in an hour?"

"Yeah, we're not far from Las Olas, so I'll head to a Starbucks or something. Just text me when you you're ready."

As I walked up the path to his house, Becks pulled off and honked at me. I approached the door and pressed the doorbell.

It didn't take long for my father to answer. He looked much the same as when I last saw him. In four years, he hadn't changed very much. His hair was a bit sparser and greyer. But he still wore the same somber expression and he still carried himself like he thought everyone was a potential enemy.

He didn't greet me with hello or even look like he wanted to hug me. He stepped aside and said, "You may as well come in. I don't want my neighbors getting in my business."

I bristled but walked past him and into the house. *Stay calm, Laney,* I reminded myself. *He's always been this way.* I waited for him to make the next move. I wasn't really sure what to do or say. I glanced around and took in the surroundings. His living room was neat though sparse. The walls had been painted a pale shade of beige, which reminded me of the house I'd grown up in. Even then he'd hated having much color on the walls.

"This is a nice place you have..." I nearly said 'Dad' but the word refused to come forward.

He didn't answer or help me make any sort of segue into a near-normal conversation. He didn't even offer me a seat, so I followed his lead. When he sat in an armchair close to the window, I moved over to the sofa and sat as well.

"I thought that, since I was visiting Aunt Cecily, I'd come by...and we could talk."

"I don't want to get into it about your mother again. I'm tired of talking about her. I get enough of that from Cecily."

"What if I think I still need to know why you left me? And why you left my mother? You never explained yourself." Well, this was off to a smashing start. I'd hoped we could ease into this but we were speeding into what was probably going to be a disappointing afternoon.

"Is that what you came here for? To make me feel bad because I chose starting over instead of you?"

His words slammed into me. I flinched but I didn't want to back down. I needed to know before I could ever let him have any sort of bond with Liv and Freya.

"I came because I wanted to find out if you were interested in seeing your granddaughters." I measured out my words, tried to keep a calm facade. "But now I'm not so sure. If you could abandon me, you'll probably just hurt and disappoint them in the end."

My father's shoulders tensed. He closed his eyes for a second and then looked off to the side. We sat there in silence. He'd said he'd chosen starting over instead of me, but I didn't see any signs of the woman he'd married after he left my mother and me. There were no family pictures in sight. What a stark contrast to my first visit with Benjamin. Benjamin had been cautious but welcoming. I'd taken the initiative but then I realized he'd been waiting all along. Alma and Henrik had given him a snapshot of Mads holding an infant Liv and he'd framed it and hung it on the living room wall. Though his apartment had been small and sparse, Benjamin had family pictures everywhere. Pictures of Mads's mother, snapshots of a towheaded Mads as a boy...and when I'd told Mads about it he'd been surprised.

"After Mom died, I thought you would change your mind and come for me." I clasped my hands to keep them from trembling. I didn't want to lose it right now. "Even when they put me in foster care, even when my social worker told me what you'd said—I was convinced you would change your mind and come for me."

Lionel remained silent, but my words were hitting their mark. His jaw tensed. He wouldn't make eye contact with me. Would he explode the way he used to? Yell at me, throw me out? Or would he sit there in stony silence and let me have my say? He leaned back in his chair, cleared his throat and gripped the armrests as though he were bracing for a physical attack. Maybe my words were like physical blows, but he'd never given me the opportunity to let him know how what had happened had affected me. Even when he invited himself to Eddy's that year for Thanksgiving, he'd only cared about how he felt.

"When Aunt Cecily found me, I thought you'd sent her. I thought she was going to drive me down to North Carolina and I was going to live with you," I continued. "But then we headed north to New York, and she told me that you still didn't want me in your life."

"It wasn't just me. Evelyn didn't want you there either."

"Was she your new wife? Is she here now? Does she want to meet me now?"

"No, she's not here." His expression grew hard. "She left me. That ought to please you. The woman I left your mother for, left me."

The news didn't make me happy. It confirmed what Cecily had said—that my father was alone; the only person he had left was Cecily. And me.

"Did you cheat on her too?" I shouldn't have asked. It was uncalled for—my slate wasn't clean. I'd cheated, even if I wasn't married. I'd cheated and I'd found Mads. I'd found the person who was meant for me. "Did you at least love her?"

"I loved your mother, I just didn't love her enough."

"What about me? Did you ever love me?"

"You make me sound like I'm a heartless man, Laney. And I was never heartless." Lionel straightened his back now, as though he were gathering his courage. Maybe he was. He had to defend himself now against whatever I needed to get out of my system in order to trust him with my daughters. "When I met Evelyn, she gave me an ultimatum—it was her or nothing. You think that's an easy choice to make? I loved that woman like there was no tomorrow, and she was telling me I could have her but not my daughter."

"And you picked her. So maybe you didn't love me enough either."

"Maybe I didn't. I could go months without thinking of you and then suddenly you'd be in my head, reminding me that I was a shit who'd left you to the wolves."

His confession cut me. I don't remember when the tears started falling, but it wasn't long before I began to cry. I should have told Becks to stay. I should have let Mads come with us. Instead I was sitting here, my face buried in my hands, silently crying in front of a man who should have protected me as a child and who'd walked away. When he stood, I thought he would come to me and comfort me, but he went past me, then returned with a box of tissues. He set them down on the side table and then returned to his armchair.

"How old are they now?"

I snatched a tissue from the box and wiped at my eyes. "Liv and Freya, you mean?" My voice shook as I spoke. I swallowed and tried to still the confusion inside of me. "Liv's four now...and Freya's going to be eight months old soon."

"You still married to him?"

"His name is Mads."

"I know his name. Are you still married to him?"

"Yes, we're still married."

"He treat you okay?"

I nodded. Even with everything we'd been through, I couldn't deny that Mads loved me, that he would never abandon me or the girls. I knew this without having to question it. Just like me, he'd longed for a family, and we'd become that for one another.

"He loves me. He loves our daughters....we had a rough couple of months, but we're working through it. And I think we'll be okay."

My father nodded. "I'm glad. I don't want you ending up like me. But Cecily told me you'd never do that. She told me how good you are with your daughters."

"Do you want to see them?"

He swiped his mouth with his palm and then nodded. "I want to meet them."

"If I let you meet them, you can't just walk away. You can't just leave them like you left me."

"Okay."

"It's that simple?"

He nodded again. "It's that simple."

CHAPTER SIXTEEN: Mads

Breathe...Gently

The hours dragged by and Laney hadn't returned. I didn't want to call or nag, but I couldn't help worrying. The last time she'd seen Lionel, she'd come away from the encounter so full of anger—at him, at me for not understanding initially...even at Eddy, who'd had no idea Lionel was even in town. I figured the only thing I could do was keep busy. I loaded the dishwasher, cleaned the bathroom, tried to read the newspaper but my mind kept wandering back to Laney and wondering if she was okay.

At one point, my iPhone rang but when I answered it was Henrik, checking to make sure I'd arrived and hoping the status of my arrival was good.

"Everything's okay," I told him as I went out onto the back porch. I wasn't really used to American houses and air-conditioning. Even though Cecily didn't have the air conditioning on full blast, it still felt too cold to me. "I'm exhausted from the flight, but everything seems okay right now."

"It's quiet—are you home alone?"

"Yeah, Cecily took Liv and Freya on an excursion, and Laney's gone to see her father."

"Really? But last time..." Henrik's voice trailed off. I could hear Eddy in the background and Henrik telling her the news. It didn't take long before she took control of the phone.

"Mads? Why aren't you with her?" Eddy demanded. She sounded agitated. I didn't blame her. I was worried too.

"She went with a friend of hers, I wanted to go with her but she said no."

Eddy groaned. "Mads, sometimes you have to take charge. And when it comes to my Uncle Lionel, you have to be there to be the buffer."

"I wanted to, but she stuck to her guns."

"Jesus Christ, you Scandinavian men kill me. Now is not the time to be rational. Get in your rental car and go to my uncle's house!"

"Eddy, she went with her friend Rebecca. I'm going to call her in a few minutes and make sure everything is okay."

"Well, at least that's something..." Eddy calmed down. "Did...was she happy to see you?"

"Yeah, she was...so were Liv and Freya...Eddy, it feels so good to be with my family again. If she'd sent me away, I don't know what I would have done."

"You would've kept trying. Just like when she was sitting the fence about leaving Niklas, you didn't give up.

Even when I was sure you would—you didn't. And you wouldn't just give up now."

"No..."

"And if you ever let her run away again, I will personally kick your ass, Mads Rasmussen."

I laughed but I was pretty sure Eddy was serious. She'd already given me a hard time about not being supportive enough—and I deserved it. I'd been an ass. "I promise, Eddy...I've learned my lesson."

"Good...I don't want see my cousin like that again. I honestly thought she was going to do something drastic. I'm glad she went to my mother. I wasn't sure what she was going to do. I did as much as I could to help, but all she wanted was you."

"I'm glad you were there for her, Eddy." I squinted against the sunlight. The heat felt good on my skin, slowly warming it after so many hours in air conditioning. "I should have been there for her...but I'm glad she has you in her corner."

We spoke a few more minutes, with Eddy finally letting Henrik have the phone again.

"So, I don't need to worry about you going through another divorce?" he joked. He was the only one who was allowed to joke about my first failed marriage.

"I don't think so." I shook my head. "She said she still loved me, she said she wanted our marriage to work. We both want it to work."

"You'll be fine," Henrik said. "Just...be more observant from now on."

By the time we ended the call, Laney and Rebecca were returning. I went to meet them, anxious to hear how it had gone. Rebecca shrugged at me and rolled her eyes skyward. "Your wife won't leave my radio stations alone," she announced as Laney opened the door on the passenger side.

I peered at Laney, hoping I'd be able to read her mood by her expression. She smiled at me, but her smile didn't quite reach her eyes. I glanced at Rebecca, hoping she'd give a sign, but she shook her head.

Laney hugged Rebecca goodbye and thanked her for going with her.

"Yoga tomorrow?" Rebecca asked as she climbed back in the car.

Laney nodded. "Most definitely. I need it."

Once we were alone, I asked Laney how it went. She took my hand as we headed back to the house. Her palm was dry against mine. I stopped before we came to the porch steps and gathered her in my arms. She trembled against me, finally giving in to all the emotions her encounter with Lionel had stirred up. I held her until her breathing steadied, stroked her neck, kissed her and murmured, "It'll be alright, *kæreste*. The girls...they have us, they have Cecily...my *farmor*, Henrik and Eddy...and my father. They have all the family they need."

She held me tighter. "He says he wants to meet the girls...I'm still not sure if I trust him."

We retreated to the sun lounger. The shade was welcome now that the afternoon sun was so strong. Laney curled into me. Her hair tickled my nose. We lay together, not saying anything, just breathing...touching.

"So tell me what happened." I slid my hand along her collarbone. Her skin was hot and damp.

She turned into my chest; her lips kissed a trail along my shoulder. I gripped her... just this was enough to ignite a spark.

"He said when my mother died, the woman he was with made him choose—her or me." Traces of bitterness still tinged her words. "And he chose her...."

"Laney, damn...I'm sorry."

"And the crazy thing is...he chose her—and she *left* him." Her hand balled into a fist. I took it in mine, massaged away the tension and unfurled her fingers. "He chose her over me...and she still left him."

I distracted her with a long kiss. I knew she needed this. I didn't want her to sink too low because of her father. He'd done enough damage.

"Maybe we shouldn't let him into our lives anymore," I suggested. "I don't want Lionel to have the chance to hurt the girls the way he hurt you."

"I just want to give him the same chance we gave Benjamin," Laney retorted. "I told my father that there were conditions that needed to be met if he wanted a relationship with his granddaughters. I'm trying to be fair...even if he doesn't deserve it."

"Are you sure, though?" Liv and Freya were too precious to both of us to ever have their lives turned upside down by a grandfather who could turn his back on them as easily as he had done to their mother. Even with my own father I'd been reluctant to have him establish any relationship with them that he could destroy with his drinking problems. "Liv and Freya—"

"He gets one chance to meet them, and if it doesn't go well, if any warning bells go off, that's it." She raised her lips to be kissed. I gladly gave her what she wanted. "One chance...just like we gave Benjamin. And if he can't rise to the occasion, then we will do what's best for Liv and Freya. And if that means a life only knowing one of their grandfathers, then so be it."

* * *

Laney made me wait. Being so near her, I wanted to touch her, taste her, be inside of her again. But she was more cautious. I could tell she felt the same—when we kissed, her kisses were just as full of longing as mine. She'd suck on my lower lip, capture it between her teeth and tease me...and god, how it made me want to drag her into the bedroom and strip her, plunge so deep into her until she screamed my name... but she told me we needed to take things a little slower. "There's still so much we need to talk about," she reminded me, when I tried to coax her into making love while we had the house to ourselves. Who knew when we'd have this chance again? No precocious four-year-old knocking on the door to inform us that she could hear Mommy making funny noises...no seven-month-old waking and crying for food or a change of diaper... but Laney shook her head and said, "We're not making love again until it feels like we've completely cleared the air."

I hoped she'd forget about this soon. We'd spent too long not making love, not reconnecting physically, but I could see her point of view. The air between us still vibrated with things unsaid. Last night, I'd been unable to restrain myself. Just to be near her, to smell the scent of her skin and to feel how her body responded when I kissed her—no, abstaining last night just hadn't been an option. I'd needed to touch and claim every part of her. I'd needed a reminder of what I'd been so close to losing. And I think Laney felt the same. As soon as we were alone, she'd begun to strip, locking me in her gaze as she peeled her tank top off and tossed it on the floor. My jaw went slack as I watched...mesmerized as she revealed inch after inch of dark skin warmed to a chocolaty brown by the sun. Her tan lines teased me...and when she unclasped her bra and let it slide to the floor, the sight of her breasts, so beautifully plump and full...her nipples already taut and aching to be sucked...my mouth went dry. All I could think was, *I need to taste her, I need...her.*

Now though, we were in her aunt's house and Laney was in the shower, and I was trying to figure out how to deal with this want when all I wanted was have more of her. I could hear the water from the power shower splattering against the tiles. Laney was singing, as she always did while she showered.

I came into the bathroom, and watched as she bowed her head down and let the stream of water pelt her skin. She looked like a water nymph, so voluptuous and tempting... God, I wanted her.

I said her name and somehow she heard me over the splattering shower stream. She lifted her head and focused on me through the steamed glass. "I thought we said we'd wait..."

"No, *you* said you'd wait...I didn't really agree." I grinned at her as I unzipped my shorts.

She smiled and rolled her eyes dramatically. "You're incorrigible, Mads."

"I'm not sure I know what that means, but it sounds good." I kicked aside my shorts and boxers, then slipped out of my shirt. "And you're tempting me."

She laughed. "Lock the door then...god forbid anyone walks in on us."

I did as she asked, then I climbed into the shower with her. I loved how her body had changed from the pregnancies. When we'd first met, she was curvy, but not in the same way as now. Now her hips were rounder, her breasts, plumper...somehow so much more luscious. And I pinned her against the wall, sucking on her nipples until she gasped, easing my hand between her legs and teasing her clit with my index finger. She moaned, her eyes closing, droplets of water trembling on her taut nipples. Her breath came out in ragged bursts as I dipped my fingers inside of her. She whispered, "Don't stop..."

I could feel her clit swelling, her inner walls squeezing my fingers, and the more her arousal heightened, the more I craved her. Laney clutched at me; she was still moaning, and the sound of her moans echoing on the tile walls sent shivers of longing through my veins. My cock was already hard, begging to be ensconced inside Laney, but I wanted to taste her before I gave in. I slid to my knees, slammed off the shower head and took possession of her. I sucked her, kissed her, slid my tongue inside her and savored each shiver, each gasp. The taste of her...oh God, the taste of her. I gripped her hip with one hand as she slung one thigh over my shoulder and held me where she wanted me. She would come soon...I could feel it building, as she tensed, then started and gasped...her fingers curled in my hair and raked my scalp and neck. Oh God...she was so wet, so swollen...and then it started...her orgasm came in waves, soft and undulating at first and I didn't stop.

And when she seemed to melt, I caught her, pulling her down onto the floor with me, letting her rest against me as she caught her breath. She laughed softly in my ear, her breathing slowing to normal...nibbled at my neck and sighed, "You're a naughty boy, Mads Rasmussen...very naughty."

I don't think she minded, though.

Later, when we were both exhausted and too lazy to do more than hold one another as we lay in bed together, Laney trailed her fingertips over the ridges of my nose as a lazy smile danced over her lips. "You were so right not to listen to me..." Her breath tickled my skin. This was what I'd missed for so many months. These moments when it was just us and we could forget about everything except for the sounds of our hearts beating in perfect rhythm.

"We needed to reconnect." I took the chance to capture her lips with mine. She giggled and dove in for another kiss. "We can talk now...if you can concentrate."

"We should...." she agreed. "And...I should tell you I quit my job."

"When...?" I tried to focus as her hand crept along my chest, moving lower and lower with each breath I took. "I thought you said they wanted you to come back early."

"They did. And I didn't want it," she said. "It was just too soon to leave Freya. And I knew if I said no, they'd play hardball."

I started doing mental calculations. If we only had my salary coming in...and that wasn't always as stable as I liked due to the nature of our projects...then I would have to start teaching at the local *højskole* again. There was no way I'd go back to Copenhagen Cryo.

"You're quiet." She drew circles on my skin with the tip of her index finger.

"I'm glad you quit—you weren't happy there. But I'm worried too..."

"Don't be...Marius and Johan quit too, and they're starting their own agency." She inched her hand lower still until her fingers were stroking the length of my cock. "And I'm going to work with them."

"When does this start?" I tried not to moan or get too distracted, but it was proving difficult. "Maybe we should stop so we can focus..."

"I'm perfectly focused," she moved her hand slowly and smiled. "I thought you'd like this..."

"I do—that's the problem."

She kept her hand still long enough to say, "I think this could work—starting up an agency with Marius and Johan. They're so good at branding and we've got enough connections that we could make enough money to support ourselves."

I set my hand over hers to stop her from moving it again. I was so hard it hurt. Damn... "Don't...move...just let me concentrate."

"I have other ideas too..."

"Yeah, I'll bet you do."

"I meant for how I can support myself," she laughed. "I'm going to write Bobbi Fox stories and sell them myself."

"Liv will love you even more for it." I laced my fingers around Laney's. "I could help with the illustrations..."

"Maybe..." she caught my lower lip again and gave it a gentle tug. "Or maybe you'll be too busy at the workshop... I thought Ingrid might like to help. She's so good at watercolors and acrylics."

She shook my hand away and climbed on top of me, straddling me without breaking her gaze. "I don't want to talk anymore, Mads..."

I let her take charge...sometimes talking was overrated.

By the time Cecily arrived home with the kids, Laney and I were secretly relieved they were too tired to do more than eat dinner and sleep. We put them to bed without mentioning the possibility of their meeting their other grandfather. Laney didn't want to bring it up if it turned out that Lionel never called. I had the feeling he would, though; so did Cecily.

Laney filled her aunt in on her meeting with Lionel as we sat together on the back porch. The night sky was heavy and wet. I was pretty sure it would rain again. Over the treetops, pale flashes of lightning flickered. I was hoping Lionel wouldn't be a constant storm on our horizon. In a way, I wanted him to change. I wanted to believe that, like Benjamin, he'd make an effort for the sake of his granddaughters. But I was skeptical, and I was not willing to expose Liv and Freya to the horrible way he'd treated Laney.

"I've often wondered if Lionel was ready to make amends," Cecily said. "When he first moved here to Florida, he would sometimes come to visit and he'd ask about you."

Laney barely moved but her eyes widened. She hadn't expected that. Neither had I. We'd grown so used to life without Lionel. Our lives in Copenhagen kept us busy enough that it wasn't often Laney even mentioned him. But maybe she simply never mentioned him to me. She confided so often in Ingrid and Eddy, I knew they were the keepers of all her secrets. Maybe she'd even spoken to my father about her relationship with Lionel.

"Do you think we should let him meet Liv and Freya?" I asked Cecily.

"A part of me wants to say yes," Cecily sighed. "He's their grandfather, even if he isn't always the most wonderful person. But I also don't want to see those girls have their hearts broken by him."

"That's what I'm concerned about, too."

"Maybe he won't call at all," Laney said. "After that time in New York, he never called. He made a scene and then he left."

"The only thing we can do is wait and see." Cecily took Laney's hand in hers. "But the decision is yours in the end. If you aren't certain, then don't open that door any further."

But we didn't have to wait very long. The next morning, we woke to a voicemail message from Lionel, letting us know he was ready to meet our daughters and wondering if he could come to dinner.

CHAPTER SEVENTEEN: Laney

Falling Into Place

I tried to stick to my normal schedule, but it was difficult. Having Mads here, I wanted to spend as much time as possible with him. We had so much lost time to make up for. But then I also wanted to continue with the Mommy and Baby yoga classes and my morning walks. I loved those moments with Freya, when she'd giggle as she tried to imitate the positions she saw me hold. And after each class, I felt as though my bond with my youngest daughter grew stronger and stronger. I looked forward to tucking her in at night or when she'd scoot over to me and climb into my lap. I knew these were things other parents took for granted, but it had taken so long for this bond to come.... I'd thought it would come as easy as it had with Liv. I'd fallen in love with her the moment I was first able to hold her. She was the sun, moon and stars... but with Freya, I'd felt empty. Only now did I feel that overwhelming love, and I hoped I could make it up to her somehow.

But for now I focused on trying to heave myself out of bed for a morning walk. Beside me, Mads slept, one arm thrown over my waist, the other clutching his pillow. He mumbled in his sleep and drew me closer. I didn't resist, though I knew I ought to get up. Instead, I nuzzled into him and closed my eyes again. I nearly fell asleep but then the bedroom door creaked open and a few seconds later Liv scrambled into the bed with us. She wriggled between us and then stuck her thumb in her mouth and drifted off again.

I pressed a kiss to her cheek. I didn't need to get up just yet. We could have a lazy morning... we had plenty of time for everything else.

When I woke again, I was alone in bed. I rolled over and hugged Mads's pillow. It still held his scent. Even when he hadn't been at the workshop for several days, the fresh, outdoorsy scent of wood resin clung to him. I breathed it in and exhaled slowly. Mads was doing breakfast duty with the girls. I could hear him trying to convince them to finish eating whatever he'd prepared. He'd probably tried to give Liv a Danish style breakfast— yoghurt with muesli and fruit, but she'd got used to having scrambled eggs and toast every day thanks to Aunt Cecily. Mads didn't lose his patience. He rarely did with Liv. I was the one who was more likely to yell if I couldn't take it anymore. But listening to how he humored her, how he tried to do Bobbi Fox's voice in an attempt to convince Liv that muesli was what foxes liked best, filled me with happiness. Mads was like the sun for me. I didn't want to go the sort of life I'd had with Niklas, so predictable, so structured and empty. I liked the chaos of our life; the only thing I wanted was for Mads to be more present. And I think he understood this now.

I stretched and finally found the energy to leave bed. In the kitchen, Freya was babbling to no one in particular, singing "mama, papa, baba, chacha..." As soon as she noticed me, she stretched out her arms to me and sang, "Mama yaya!"

I lifted her out of the highchair and gave her a noisy kiss, which she loved. My sweet little Freya—would my father love her as much as I did? Would he treasure Liv and her the way that Mads and I did? Mads was still talking to Liv, still making Bobbi Fox dance around the untouched bowl of muesli and yogurt. Liv was pointedly ignoring him and singing "What Does the Fox Say?" Mads tickled her chin, but—even though she giggled—she wouldn't be swayed. She wanted eggs.

"Fine," Mads surrendered. "I'll make eggs. But when we're home again you won't have eggs every day."

"Yes, I will," Liv retorted. "I am American girl too."

"You are," Mads agreed. "But you're also my little Liv, who is a Danish girl."

"Danish girls like eggs too."

"Liv...won't you eat the yogurt and muesli?" I sat down beside her, bouncing a giggling Freya on my knee. "We can have eggs tomorrow."

Liv wrinkled her nose as she considered this. "Will we have *korv* too?"

"Yes, we'll have sausages. And then we'll go to the beach, all of us."

"Okay!" And with that Liv began to eat her cereal while she balanced Bobbi Fox on her knees.

The relieved expression on Mads's handsome face was enough thanks. He scratched his head as he watched Liv gobble down the muesli. The rest of our breakfast passed without stress. Liv was happy; Freya gurgled on my lap while I ate the plate of eggs and bacon Mads had prepared for me. Mads sat across from me, reading Danish news on his iPad while sipping his coffee. Liv slipped out her chair and went to him. He helped her into his lap and whispered to her. She nodded, giggling. When they both began singing "What Does the Fox Say?" Freya clapped her hands and tried to sing along. This was my family, and I loved them so much...how did I ever think I could live without this?

Lionel popped into my head, unwanted just then. I still needed to figure out to handle his coming over. Would he be good to my girls? Would he be gentle with them or would he be as acerbic and dismissive as he'd often been with me when I was a child? My mother had tried to shield me from the worst of it, but it still cut deep. The worst thing was understanding this and not being quite clever enough to realize that nothing I did was going to change how he felt about me.

"Laney?" Mads had stopped singing, though Liv was still singing. He watched me over the top of our daughter's head. "Are you okay?"

I nodded quickly. "Just thinking, that's all."

"Is it Lionel?"

"I was wondering if he'll love them like we do."

"No," Mads retorted. He set aside his iPad. "He can't possibly love them as we do. He'll have to figure out his own way."

Freya gurgled and slapped her palms on the tabletop. She and Liv laughed together, both of them thumping the table and serenading us with "papa-mama-papa." If Lionel couldn't figure out a way to love his granddaughters, then he didn't deserve any further chances to affect their lives.

* * *

I decided not to question Mads's sartorial choices for the girls. I knew what he was doing. He wanted to make sure Lionel understood we weren't making a huge effort here, that this was an ordinary evening and he just happened to be included in it. He was right. What was the point of getting Liv and Freya dressed up for a normal dinner? Any change in their routine and they'd sense that something wasn't quite right and were likely to go into tantrum mode. I wanted everything to be easy, at least when it came to the girls meeting their grandfather. I didn't want to worry about whether Liv managed to pour salsa sauce down the front of her linen romper or if Freya smashed strawberries on her pants. Mads had bathed them, brushed their hair as best he could and dressed them both in their favorite T-shirts and shorts.

"They're comfortable," Mads explained when he brought the girls outside, "and these outfits can go right in the washing machine in the morning."

"Who knew you were so practical?" I teased as I set the last place mat on my aunt's patio dining table. We'd been dining al fresco most nights since we arrived and figured the weather was fine enough for a barbecue. Cecily had already wheeled her sun umbrella out of the garage and opened it so its canopy would protect us from the late day sun. Most of the food was ready—I'd roasted some tomatoes, baked cornbread and made a pasta salad and a mixed green salad while Cecily marinated the fish and meat that we'd toss on the grill as soon as my father arrived. The only thing missing was dessert, which Mads and the girls were taking care of—they were on their way to the local bakery to pick up cupcakes and ice cream.

"I had to learn fast," he grinned and nodded at our daughters. "They run you ragged otherwise."

I couldn't help smiling. Now that he'd been here a few days, he understood how high energy two toddlers could be. He was used to only doing the fun things with them and having to deal with the everyday part of being a parent was giving him some perspective.

He managed to get Freya in the stroller and then he and the girls headed off on their dessert mission. Once they were gone, my aunt came back outside with two ice buckets and bottles of chilled sparkling water.

"Lionel just called," she said as she set the ice buckets on the table. "He'll be here in five minutes."

I let this sink in. He was actually coming. I'd mused that perhaps he wouldn't show up. I was used to that from my father. He didn't show up for my high school and college graduations despite my inviting him; he never called on birthdays or even acknowledged that I existed except for when he was suddenly reminded of his own mortality.

"Don't be nervous, kiddo." My aunt enveloped me in one of those hugs that reminded me of my mother. She kissed my cheek and patted my back. "I'm here, Mads will be back shortly. We're your champions. And if Lionel starts acting up, I'm sending his ass home."

"I just want him to love..."

"Honey, if he doesn't fall in love with those little girls the moment he lays eyes on them, then he doesn't deserve a place in their lives."

"I think I'll need a glass of wine to get through this," I joked. "Or maybe a bottle or two."

"I've got some rosé in the fridge," Cecily kissed my cheek one more time. "We may as well bring it out. Though I'm sure we'll need the stronger stuff by the end of the evening."

My father arrived just as Mads and the girls were returning from their dessert run. Lionel had just opened the garden gate when Liv saw him and said in a very loud voice, "Papa, who is that big man?"

Mads took it in stride. He shook Lionel's hand and then informed Liv that this was her other grandfather, Lionel.

My father's usual stony expression softened as he crouched down to greet Liv and Freya. "That's right. I'm your...how is it you say in Danish? *Morfar*? Your mother's father?"

Liv nodded, though she didn't go over to him. She'd slung her arm around Mads's leg and was leaning against him.

"Lionel, this is Liv..." Mads reached down and cupped Liv's shoulder. "And this little one is Freya."

I moved forward and greeted my father, but he was still regarding my daughters. Mads caught my eye and winked at me. Liv looked as though she were gearing up for a weird question. She was the master of those and when it came I couldn't help chuckling.

"*Morfar*, do you like foxes?"

"Foxes? I don't think I've ever met any." Lionel was still crouching at Liv and Freya's level. "Do you know any foxes I should meet?"

Liv nodded. "Bobbi Fox! She's my best friend. Do you want to meet her?"

"Is she a nice fox?"

"She's the best fox, *morfar*. She's friends with my *far-far* too." And then, as Lionel stood to his full height, Liv left Mads's side and grabbed her grandfather's hand. "Come, I'll show you Bobbi Fox."

And that was it. All the tension melted. I watched how my father let Liv lead him inside. Cecily trailed behind them while Mads and I took care of the grill. Freya watched with wide, curious eyes from her comfortable spot in the stroller.

By the time they returned, the fish and steaks were ready. I'd lit citronella candles to ward off any mosquitoes, and Liv...well, she had her *morfar* wrapped around her finger.

CHAPTER EIGHTEEN: Mads

With Every Heartbeat

Over the next few days, Lionel came by often—to spend time with Liv and Freya, to make amends with Laney. Sometimes he made awkward conversation with me, but more often than not he concentrated on his granddaughters. I didn't take it personally. In some ways he was like my own father—stiff, distant...uncomfortable with emotions. And to him, I was just the foreign man his estranged daughter had married. He was never rude to me. But he didn't seem to know what to say to me, and honestly I wasn't quite sure what we could talk about other than my daughters and my wife. Laney tried to get him interested in my furniture making and design. She showed him the collective's website and the gallery of images from our finished projects, but Lionel only nodded and said, "Looks good."

His interest in Liv and Freya gave me hope. If he could be this attentive with our daughters, perhaps he could begin to open up more with Laney. Sometimes I eavesdropped on them while I checked my email. Lionel was trying. He stopped fighting Laney when she asked him about his marriage with her mother. Laney would get exasperated with him and walk away. I'd convince her to go back and hear him out. By the time she'd return to the garden to sit with him and listen, Liv had often commandeered her grandfather's attention and was making him laugh with her crazy dances and songs. And if Liv's songs didn't work, a giggle from Freya was enough to make Lionel melt a little more.

By Friday, I knew I needed to check in with the guys at the workshop. While Laney and Cecily took Liv to the beach, I took care of Freya—she'd got sunburned they day before and was cranky—and had a Skype call with Jonas and Anton. They'd just come back from Milan and were excited about the reception they'd received.

"The Italians loved the original designs from the Vesterbrogade Project." Jonas sounded as excited as a little kid with a new toy. "We made some good contacts here—another hotel is interested in our work."

"That's great news." I gave them the thumbs-up. "Is it an Italian hotel?"

Before Jonas could answer, Freya began to cry. I told him to hold on and went to fetch her. Her shoulders were still red from being out in the sun too long and the bridge of her nose was still an angry red. I'd have to put some after-sun cream and aloe vera gel on the burns soon. I was careful with her as I picked her up. Tears were still streaming down her face but she smiled for me and threw her chubby arms around my neck.

When I returned to my computer, Freya rested her head on my shoulder and sang softly to herself. Jonas continued to regale me with news from Milan. Then Anton took over and started filling me in on the latest with Benny. I groaned on hearing her name. "Is she still causing problems?"

"She tried, she thought we ought to pay her extra salary since we ended her contract early."

"What did Anoushka say?"

"She said that since it was an internship, the only thing we owed Benny was her last month's salary." Anton waved to Freya, but she was already falling asleep on my shoulder. "How's the little one?"

"Sunburned. Wouldn't stay still long enough for me to get any sunscreen on her."

"Poor Freya...everything okay there? With you and Laney?"

"Better...I think we're back on track." I gently patted Freya's back. "We've been talking everything through, spending time together and taking care of the kids together."

"You think you'll be home soon?"

"I'm not sure," I admitted. I wanted to get back to work, but I also needed more time away, enjoying my family and not being distracted by the weight of so many professional commitments. "Laney and I, we need a bit more time."

"No worries, we'll keep everything going here. Jonas, Morten and I are all in your corner, you know. We know you're happier with Laney than you'd ever be without her."

"Thanks, it's good to know you guys have got my back."

"By the way, Ole and the Vesterbrogade group seem to like the latest revisions." Anton glanced over his shoulder. "Actually, when they heard the Italians were crazy about the original designs, they started talking about going back to it."

I laughed. Of course they wanted it again. All it took was someone else wanting it more.

Once Anton and I rang off, I took Freya into the bathroom and cooled off her skin with a cold compress. The aloe vera gel came next. Freya whimpered at first but as the gel soothed away the heat she settled down and a tiny smile emerged again. I hated seeing her like this. How did Laney deal with this all the time? All I knew was I wanted to make everything better for my little girl.

She was growing so fast—just yesterday she'd managed to pull herself up on her own and balance for a few moments. Laney and I had watched, mesmerized, as our youngest daughter planted her hands onto the sofa cushion to brace herself and try to stand. In a few days she would be eight months old. Would she be an early bloomer and begin walking before she was even ten months old? Or would she be more like Liv, who'd taken her time about walking and explored every inch of the apartment crawling or scooting, only to take us by surprise on her first birthday by standing and taking off almost immediately in a wobbly run.

After a sleepless night thanks to her sunburn, Freya was more subdued than usual, which was understandable. Hell, I was pretty exhausted too. If anything I wanted to take a nap and I'd barely been out of bed for more two or three hours. Picking up Freya again, I asked her, "What do you think, *lille ven*? Shall we take a nap?"

My daughter yawned, her sleepy green eyes struggling to remain open. We retraced the path to the bedroom Laney and I had been sharing. The bedroom faced the back garden and was shaded by most of the morning sun thanks to the lush canopy of a marbleberry tree. It cast swaying shadows on the wall as a breeze caught its branches. Freya and I watched the shadows dance. She giggled and pointed at the tree. I kept my arm protectively around her as I began to drift off. It wasn't long until even Freya settled down and her tiny sighs let me know she'd fallen asleep.

The air conditioner's hum formed a cloud of white noise that lulled me even deeper into sleep. Freya planted her thumb in her mouth. I wondered if she was dreaming of penguins. *Don't grow up too quickly*, I thought as my eyelids grew heavy. *Stay my baby girl for just a little while longer.*

* * *

Freya and I spent the rest of the morning napping, which probably wasn't very smart, but we needed it. When she finally woke up, she was happier and in a playful mood. I took her outside but made sure she was in the shade. Her unruly curls spiraled in every direction as she played with her DuPlo blocks. I'd spread a blanket on the grass and made a sunshade by stringing up another blanket between two trees. While she played, I lay on the blanket beside her and finished reading the novel Laney had given me. It wasn't often that Freya and I had so much time alone together. I set aside the book. I couldn't concentrate anyway, so I sat up and helped her build, loving how her eyes lit up with delight as she handed me blocks and I stacked them beside the wobbly towers she'd already constructed.

We were so lost in our own little world, we didn't hear my phone ringing. I grabbed it just before it transferred the caller to my voicemail.

My father's voice startled me. "When can you come home, son?"

"What's wrong? Is it *farmor*?" Freya abandoned her blocks as soon as she heard "*farmor.*"

"She's had a stroke." Benjamin's voice shook as he spoke. "The doctors say she'll recover, but she is asking for you and for Laney."

My heart was beating so hard I felt like I couldn't breathe. "I'll come. Of course I'll come."

"Good, I'll tell her. I'm on my way back to the hospital. Henrik and Edwina are with her now," he added. "Will Laney come as well?"

"Yes, I think so. She loves *farmor*, she'll want to see her."

"So it's better between you?"

"It is. It's much better. I think we found each other again."

"Good, good. Your *farmor* will be pleased."

"Was she alone when it happened?"

"No, Edwina was with her, helping her in the garden. She made sure Alma made it to the hospital quickly. She's a smart cookie."

Freya chanted "farma" at me. I ruffled her hair as my father and I ended our call. I had to go back. I needed to see with my own eyes that my grandmother was okay. As silly as it sounded, I'd never thought much about the possibility of a life that didn't include my grandmother. I knew she was getting older, that her memory wasn't as good as it had been. One day my grandmother wouldn't be around. I was just glad that day wasn't today.

"Of course we're going home," Laney said as soon as I told her the news. "Alma needs us."

While she packed, I called the airlines and arranged our flight home. It wasn't the way I wanted us to go home together, but we couldn't always control these things. Cecily kept the girls occupied for us while we arranged everything. Henrik called at one point to let me know he could pick us up from the airport. I gave him our flight details. Tomorrow afternoon, we'd be on our way back to Denmark. And after we checked on my grandmother and made sure she was okay, we could start the next stage of our lives together.

CHAPTER NINETEEN: Laney

Home

"*Morfar*!"

Mads and I were jolted out of our much-needed sleep by Liv's excited shrieks. We'd been up most of the night discussing whether it was time for Alma to move to an assisted living complex. Neither of us wanted her to be own her own anymore, but we also didn't want her to have to leave her home. We still hadn't really come to any decision by the time we fell asleep.

"Mommy, Mommy! *Morfar* is here! Come!" It wasn't long until Liv was at our door, issuing commands.

"I'm coming, sweetie. Tell *morfar* I'll be there in five minutes..."

A bleary-eyed Mads rolled onto his side. He yawned and reached for me. "Do we have to get up?"

I nodded. "He probably wants to say goodbye since we're leaving today."

While Mads struggled out of bed, I went into the bathroom and tried to make myself as presentable as possible. I managed to tame my hair into submission and then change from my pajamas into a pair of shorts and a polo shirt. My father was already in the garden with Cecily and the girls. He and Liv were watering the flower beds while my aunt pruned her clematis and passion flowers.

I greeted my father with a wave and said, "You're here early."

"I wanted to spend time with my grandbabies before they head back across the ocean." Lionel replied as he held the hose steady for Liv. She squealed with delight when a bumblebee hovered over the stream of water. "And I wanted to make sure we had a chance to say goodbye."

"Lionel, you make it sound like you won't see the child again," Cecily chided as she snipped off another dead flower head. "She'll be back, won't you, Laney?"

"Absolutely," I said. "Later this year. We need to make sure everything is okay with Mads's grandmother, get her situated once she's home from the hospital."

Freya was pushing herself up in what looked like one of the yoga positions we'd practiced. I watched her plant her feet on the grass and slowly, wobbly raise herself upwards. She stretched her arms out towards me. I held mine open and waited, practically holding my breath. Lionel set down the water hose aside and smiled as he, too, watched Freya trying to find her balance. She was only eight months old—wasn't this too early for her to start trying to walk? But I'd seen how she watched Liv running back and forth...of course she wanted to keep up with her older sister. Liv clapped her hands and ran to Freya's side. She took Freya's hand and spoke to her little sister as she tried to balance. Freya tottered a bit but found her balance again. Behind me, Mads came out on the porch. I heard his sharp intake of breath as we all watched and waited to see what Freya would do next. She took one uncertain step forward, planted her foot in the grass and wobbled again, landed on her rump and giggled.

"Come, Freya," Liv insisted as she helped her little sister stand. "We are going to walk!"

"Don't rush her," Lionel said. "Baby girl's got to find her way."

"If she walks, she is a big girl then," Liv said. "And then we can play."

Freya stood to her feet again with Liv's help. She swayed, then seemed to find her balance. She took one step, waited and giggled. Then she took another. She landed on her rump again.

"They grow up so fast." Lionel scooped up Freya and kissed the top of her head. Mads and I reached for one another's hands. His fingers slid between mine. Our daughters laughed together and sang for their grandfather.

I hoped this peace we'd found would not evaporate when we returned to Copenhagen. Mads leaned in and kissed my neck, his lips skimming my skin and setting off tiny sparks throughout my body. We sat like this for a long while, the sound of our daughters' laughter filling our ears, my aunt's gentle teasing of my father making me smile.

We were surrounded by love. And this was how I'd always wanted my life to be.

A YEAR LATER: Laney

At the Beach

It was hard to imagine that this time last year was so awful for us. Mads and I had weathered a storm I'd initially thought we'd never survive. But now we were back in Florida, celebrating our fifth anniversary with our daughters. We'd exchanged houses with my aunt—she was in Copenhagen visiting Eddy and Henrik and spending the summer with her twin grandbabies.

Coming back felt right—we'd mended our marriage here. Freya and I forged our bond here.

Today, though, we focused on spending a relaxing day at the beach. We'd invited Rebecca and her daughters to join us. Peyton and Lorelei were building a sandcastle with Liv. Under our sun shades, Rebecca and I pondered whether we'd dare to take a dip. Mads was already in the water with Freya, hopping around and laughing with her. I shaded my eyes with my hand and watched as they frolicked. My husband was golden brown from so many hours spent in the sun, taking our daughters to the playground, working in the garden at his grandmother's house which she'd deeded to us now that she'd moved into a nursing home nearby. I watched him and felt my love for him swelling inside me, quickening and taking hold, reminding me that I was adored, that I adored him.

"You two made it through," Rebecca said with a grin.

"We did," I agreed. "I'm glad we did...I never wanted to consider how it would be live a life without him."

"You've renewed my faith in love." Rebecca dug her toes in the sand. "In fact, I've got a date tonight."

"Tell all! Who's the lucky guy?"

"Wilson, the new guy who comes to Baby & Me yoga classes. Well, he's a single parent too. We started chatting a few weeks ago... and he asked me out yesterday."

"Morning walk tomorrow for a post-date review?" I asked. Mads and Freya were just emerging from the water now and heading toward us. "Or...should we plan for the afternoon?"

"Morning is good. I'm taking this slowly." Rebecca reached for our communal bottle of sunscreen. She called for our daughters to come and get another layer of it. "I rushed before, and I don't want to make that mistake again."

Peyton came over and claimed the sunscreen bottle. "I'll make sure Lorelei and Liv put some on," she said.

"Thanks, Peyton." Once she returned to the younger girls, I said to Rebecca, "I have some news I'm going to give Mads tonight."

"What's that?"

"I'm pregnant again..."

Rebecca gasped. "I'm so happy for you!"

I smiled at her. "We always said we wanted to have three or four kids... and, well, things have been so good between us."

"I can tell. I see how he watches you when you're not paying attention," Rebecca said.

Mads and Freya stopped by the burgeoning sandcastle. He made sure the girls applied enough sunscreen and reapplied it for Freya and then for himself. He laughed at something Peyton said then strode over to us. Grains of sand flecked his tanned skin.

"Do you think you'll come back next summer?"

I nodded. "I think so. I think we'll be back every summer."

Get a sneak peek at the first chapter of *Maybe Tomorrow*,

coming July 2015.

CHAPTER ONE: EDDY

The End

It ended just as quickly as it began.

He came home and said he didn't love me anymore, didn't think we had any future, not together. And as the words rushed out of his mouth, I stood very still, my arms folded across my chest, and waited for the truth to finally come.

I knew my lips had pulled into a thin, grim line. I was biting in the words I wanted to spit out at him. "Who have you fucked this time?" or "Can't you keep your cock in your pants?" but I held back and focused on the splotch of red wine on his shirt and told myself this was okay. I didn't need him to feel complete. I don't think I'd ever felt complete with him. He was just a boy pretending to be a man. A beautiful boy, but a boy all the same.

"Say something, Eddy." Andreas was nervous. He kept standing, pacing, and then throwing himself back into the same armchair. Under the tan his cheeks and neck burned red.

"What exactly do you want me to say?"

"You must have something you want to say. I just told you I don't love you anymore."

"Fine, I think we should sell the apartment."

"What?"

"Actually, it was mostly my money that went into this apartment," I surmised. "My down payment of...half a million kronor was it? I was the one who sold her apartment so we could move in together."

"You want to talk money?"

"Well, we're splitting up, aren't we?" I sank into the armchair opposite his and crossed my legs. I kept my voice even and light. "Since you don't love me and we have no future, why should we still share this apartment?"

"We bought it together-"

"How much money did you bring to the table?"

Andreas licked his lips and shrugged. He mumbled an "I don't know" but wouldn't make eye contact with me. We both knew the truth.

"I hope your new girlfriend has a place you can move into."

"What makes you think there is someone else?"

"With you, there's always someone else. I recognize the pattern, sweetie."

It never changed with him. We'd had a good run these last few months but I'd sensed he would get restless again. And this time I wasn't ready to forgive and forget.

"Eddy, we can't just..."

"Yes, actually, we can. You remember the last time you cheated on me? You said you would move out if it happened again."

"But, Eddy, be realistic."

"I am being realistic. And that's exactly what I want you to do. Move. And we'll sell this place. You put thirty percent into it, and that's exactly what you'll get."

He shook his head and then launched out of the chair and stormed out of the room.

The knot in my stomach unraveled slowly. But the bitter taste of another failed relationship...that took even longer to disappear.

When he left, the apartment seemed to breathe out a long sigh of relief, as if it had been waiting for this very moment. In a few days it would be Midsummer and the evening sky was still full of light.

I wandered through every room, making sure he'd taken everything that was his. I didn't want to wake to another day of being reminded that Andreas and I had shared this apartment.

I kept telling myself I was okay with this, and I was. I didn't want to have to grin and bear it again. But there was that nagging little voice that I could just barely hear over the super positive "I am a strong, independent woman" mantra on repeat in my mind—that naggy, snarky little bitch who reveled in reminding me, "This is the third time you're the one left alone."

"Shut up, bitch.." I muttered.

"Sorry?"

I'd forgotten about the real estate agent, who was also going from room to room casting an eye on all the renovations we'd done as she calculated the apartment's market value. She flashed a tight little smile at me. It was almost as tight as the skirt and blouse she wore.

"I'm just talking to myself," I assured her and then reached for my vibrating iPhone.

Another call from Andreas. I pressed reject and set my phone back on the windowsill.

"Well, your apartment will definitely be a hot commodity," she said. "An apartment this size and in this neighborhood...it'll fetch a pretty penny."

I nodded. I already knew this. It was one of the reasons I'd convinced Andreas that we should move to this part of Kungsholmen. From the living room and dining room, there was a perfect view of Norr Mälarstrand and the glittering waters of Lake Mälaren. We had a balcony that stretched the entire length of the apartment and, with all of the plants and flowers in bloom it would look inviting enough that even the most jaded Stockholmer would want to live here.

"How much do you think it's worth?"

"We're looking at...eight million kronor at least, and that's before the bidding would start."

"So we should start with an asking price of eight million?"

"At least." Her blonde head bobbed up and down excitedly. "Five rooms...a king's balcony, two walking closets..."

"Walk-in closets," I corrected.

"Sorry?"

"They're not called walking closets. The closets don't have legs. They can't go anywhere."

She clutched her iPad and barked out a nervous laugh. "Of course! Ha-ha! Whoever heard of a closet with feet!"

I put her out of her misery. "When can we say it's on the market?"

"We can list it starting on Monday. Is that too soon?"

"Couldn't we make it sooner?"

"I'm sorry, but that's as soon as we can do it."

"Fine," I conceded. "Monday it is. And...if we get a good enough bid so that I can avoid any open house, that's fine."

"Are you sure?"

"Absolutely. I want to sell this as quickly as possible."

"What will you do then?"

Behind her was a framed vintage print of the Empire State Building. Andreas had hated it but it was the one image in the apartment that reminded me of home. And right now, I wished I was in the gritty, muggy, crowded embrace of home.

I smiled at Petra the perky real estate agent. "I'm moving back to New York."

I signed the paperwork and Petra congratulated me on making the right choice of her real estate agency before she finally left.

I walked out onto the balcony and breathed in the lavender-scented air before any of the exhaust of passing cars drifted up to me. It was one of the perks of living on the top floor of the building. I would miss this view. I would miss this apartment but I couldn't stay here. It was too big for one person and, even if I met someone else, I didn't want them to walk into a place that had been the scene of so many arguments, of so much disappointment. It would surely taint any attempts I might make at starting over.

But New York. I could move back. There was nothing holding me in Stockholm anymore. Andreas and I had dissolved our business partnership as swiftly as we'd ended our relationship. I shivered and pulled my sweater closer around me. If Laney were still here, I would have considered staying. But she was in Copenhagen now, and she was so blissfully happy it was enough to make your teeth ring. I would have been super jealous if I didn't love her so much.

For now, though, I needed to focus on my life. I couldn't begrudge my cousin for her happiness. And maybe, if I was lucky, I'd find my own Happily Ever After, even if I didn't believe in that bullshit.

Acknowledgements

To everyone who helped make sure that *Maybe Forever* become a reality—you are all rock stars!

First of all, I'd like to thank Tord for all of his patience while I was writing and revising. Thank you for taking care of all the things I forget when I am in the zone. You know you're my muse. You always will be.

To Xio Axelrod—I think you may love Laney and Mads even more than I do! ;-) Thanks for our weekend chat sessions on Facebook and for helping me tweak the plot when I was losing the thread.

To Kim Kane, even though we haven't had a chance to meet as often as we like, our gab sessions help so much! You are an amazing writing buddy and writer!

To all of the readers, bloggers and reviewers who've helped spread the word about *Maybe Baby*, *Maybe Tonight*, Laney and Mads! Thank you so much for all of your support! You chicas are awesome!

To the Matera Brainstormers, thanks for helping me through plot conundrums and moments of doubt. Can't wait to see you all again!

Renata Queiroz Hansen, Andreas Hansen and Leonardo "Little Man" Hansen, for many great times in Copenhagen. And, Andreas, thanks for answering all my weird questions about Danish men. :-)

To the staff at the Hotel Kong Arthur in Copenhagen, for helping to inspire Laney and Mads's love affair. I've now worked on four books (*Maybe Baby, Maybe Tonight, Maybe Forever* and the upcoming *Maybe Tomorrow*) during my stays there. Thanks for making every stay so comfortable and so inspiring. And yes, you do serve the world's best gin & tonics. Tord still swears by them.

To Christina Plöen, thank you so much for being such a wonderful friend, for our evening chats at Knut, and for our Yngsjö visits every year. Looking forward to more inspiration, stargazing and enjoying the moonrise over the Bay of Hanö!

And finally, to my mom, Barbara Golden, you know how much I love you, Mom! :-)

About the Author

Kim Golden is a native of Philadelphia, PA. She is the author of *The Melanie Chronicles*, *Linger: a short story*, *Choose Me*, *Snowbound*, *Maybe Baby* and *Maybe Tonight.* She lives and works in Stockholm, Sweden. Find out more about Kim, her writing, and her latest NaNoWrimo project at kim-golden.com. And check out what she's reading at kimtalksbooks.com.

If you enjoyed reading *Maybe Forever*, please drop Kim a line at kimtalksbooks@gmail.com , tell all your friends, or write a review on Goodreads, Kobo, BN.com, ARe, iTunes Bookstore or Amazon.

Connect with Kim

You can connect with Kim on Facebook, Twitter, Google+, Goodreads, Tsü, Tumblr and Pinterest. Don't forget to sign up for her newsletter for the latest news, exclusive teasers and giveaways.

More books by Kim Golden

Maybe series

Maybe Baby

Maybe Tonight: a novella

Maybe Tomorrow

(coming July 2015)

Other Titles

Snowbound

Choose Me: a novella

Linger: a short story

The Melanie Chronicles

30 Days, 30 Stories

(Wattpad exclusive)

Lightning Source UK Ltd.
Milton Keynes UK
UKOW01f0922310816

281877UK00002B/85/P